Dialogue of deat

"You guys need a hand?" David McCarter asked Keio Ohara. At last the shooting had stopped and the smoke had cleared.

"I was about to ask you the same question," the Japanese replied.

"Everything seems under control downstairs," McCarter said.

"Any prisoners?"

"Nobody asked us to take any," the Englishman grunted. "Is Rafael with your blokes?"

"No," Keio said.

"And I didn't see him downstairs," McCarter said tensely. "Dammit, where is he then?"

In an alley outside, Colonel Heinrich Müller towered over Rafael Encizo, his Luger aimed at the Cuban's heart....

> "The hardest-hitting, highest caliber he-man writing ever."
>
> —*Stag*

PHOENIX FORCE

AN EXECUTIONER SERIES

Ultimate Terror

Gar Wilson

A GOLD EAGLE BOOK FROM

WORLDWIDE

TORONTO • NEW YORK • LONDON • PARIS
AMSTERDAM • STOCKHOLM • HAMBURG
ATHENS • MILAN • TOKYO • SYDNEY

First edition January 1984

ISBN 0-373-61309-1

Special thanks and acknowledgement to
William Fieldhouse for his contributions to this work.

Copyright © 1984 by Worldwide Library.
Philippine copyright 1984. Australian copyright 1984.

All rights reserved. Except for use in any review, the
reproduction or utilization of this work in whole or in part
in any form by any electronic, mechanical or other means,
now known or hereafter invented, including xerography,
photocopying and recording, or in any information storage
or retrieval system, is forbidden without the permission
of the publisher, Worldwide Library, 225 Duncan Mill Road,
Don Mills, Ontario, Canada M3B 3K9.

All the characters in this book have no existence outside the
imagination of the author and have no relation whatsoever to
anyone bearing the same name or names. They are not even
distantly inspired by any individual known or unknown to the
author, and all the incidents are pure invention.

The Worldwide Library trademark consisting of the words
GOLD EAGLE is registered in the United States Patent
Office and in the Canada Trade Marks Office. The Gold Eagle
design trademark, the Executioner series design trademark,
the Phoenix Force design trademark, the globe design
trademark, and the Worldwide design trademark consisting
of the word WORLDWIDE in which the letter "O" is
represented by a depiction of a globe are trademarks
of Worldwide Library.

Printed in Canada

PROLOGUE

"Mission accomplished," Staff Sergeant Harlon Johnson muttered as he absentmindedly gazed out the window of the truck and watched the Bavarian scenery.

"How's that, Sarge?" Private First Class Jed Turner inquired, chomping on three sticks of chewing gum as he spoke, his Alabama drawl pulling on the words. Turner's eyes remained fixed on the narrow, dirt road.

"I said we accomplished our mission," Johnson repeated dryly. "We delivered three adding machines and four typewriters for repair at Ansbach and picked up about a ton of TA-Fifty field gear for the troopies. Some mission, huh?"

"Least nobody's shooting at us," Turner replied with a shrug.

"Yeah," Johnson growled.

Harlon Johnson almost wished someone was shooting at them. Twelve years before, fresh out of high school, Harlon had joined the army, eager to go to Vietnam and earn himself a chest full of medals. But American forces were being pulled out of Southeast Asia by the time Johnson finished basic combat training. He had never seen combat, and this gnawed at his guts.

"Hell, Sarge," Turner began, turning the steering wheel deftly as the truck took a bend in the road. "Being a supply sergeant ain't so bad, is it? I don't mind being in supply. It might not be too exciting, but it ain't all that hard."

"Not for *you*," Johnson complained. "You're a truck driver. I'm the one who has to make the battery commander and the first sergeant happy. Then I've gotta worry about getting supplies to the troops and the other sections in the battery as well as getting all that office crap taken care of so the goddamn big boys stay off my ass." Johnson shook his head in dismay. "It just isn't what I figured soldiering would be like, that's all."

"You're a good supply sergeant," Turner said.

"Sure, kid," Johnson sighed, aware that Turner did not understand what was eating at him. He was not quite sure himself.

The sergeant fished a pack of cigarettes from his field jacket as he studied Turner's youthful face. "Turner, how old are you?"

"Nineteen," the driver replied. "I'll be twenty in a couple months."

"That's about how old I was when I first joined the Green Machine." Johnson lit a cigarette. "You plan to re-up?"

"I don't know." Turner shrugged. "Kinda figure that'll depend on what sort of jobs are available on the outside, you know. If the economy is still screwed up, I might re-up for a couple more years.''

''What'll you do if there's another war?'' Johnson asked.

''Jesus, Sarge.'' Turner risked taking his eyes from the road to stare at Johnson. ''You don't figure that's gonna happen, do you?''

''Of course it's going to happen,'' the sergeant said. ''The United States will get into another war pretty soon. It's overdue, believe me. I'm surprised we didn't wind up in the middle of that Falkland Islands crap a while back. Just watch. We'll end up fighting somewhere.''

''I sure hope that don't happen,'' the Pfc said, turning his attention back to the road. ''I don't want nobody shootin' at me or.... Oh, shit.''

A brown-and-white cow stood in the middle of the road a hundred yards from the truck. Turner immediately hit the brake. Johnson cursed as the sudden stop tossed him toughly into the dashboard. He hit the button of the glove compartment and the diminutive door popped open. A cluster of road maps, a flashlight and a couple dozen gum wrappers spilled into his lap.

''Jesus, Turner,'' the sergeant snapped. ''You damn near got us killed. Where the hell did that damn animal come from anyway? I didn't think there were any farms around here.''

''Must be, Sarge,'' Turner answered simply

as he popped open the door and hopped out of the cab. "Ain't no need to fret none. I'll get this cow outta the way so we can get back to Ralston Barracks before chow time."

"I have a lot of confidence in your ability to handle cows, Turner," Johnson remarked. "I've seen some of the girls you go out with."

"I like 'em hefty," Turner admitted with a grin. "Gives a man more to hold on to."

"Just don't fall in love," Johnson urged as the youth headed toward the cow.

Pfc Turner approached the animal, calling to her in a soothing voice. He knew about cows because he had been raised on a farm.

"What the hell?" he said as he stared down at the chain that extended from a brass ring in the cow's nose to a thick wooden stake driven into the ground.

"Come on, Turner," Johnson shouted. "Just get that four-legged milk machine off the road. You can come back and ask her for a date later."

"She's staked out, Sarge," the Pfc explained. "Why would somebody do that?"

"Staked out?" The sergeant's brow crinkled. Something was strange. An almost dormant sixth sense began to throb a warning in his subconscious.

Then he remembered where he had read about staked-out animals—they were used for bait. A goat is staked out by big-game hunters to lure tigers or leopards out of the bush in India.

But Turner and Johnson were not in India. They were in twentieth-century West Germany. Why stake a cow in the middle of an obscure dirt road? What was the bait for?

"Holy shit," Johnson whispered as the realization of a human trap struck home. "Turner. Get back...."

A figure emerged from the tree line and stepped onto the road behind the cow. The man wore a flannel shirt and overalls, and his blond hair was precisely combed. Johnson was certain the stranger's granite face and cold blue eyes did not belong to a friendly Bavarian farmer. Turner, however, failed to notice the threat in the man's expression.

"Howdy," the Pfc said. "Is this your cow? *Ist das...?*"

Turner was still trying to think of the German word for "cow" when the man raised his right arm. A thick metal sausage stared at Turner long enough for the Pfc to see a black hole at the end of the cylinder.

Phut. Phut. The silencer spit harshly.

Two bullets tore into the young American's chest. Turner staggered backward, his eyes wide with alarm and pain.

His heart exploded and he fell to the ground—dead.

Sergeant Johnson was startled. What was going on? Why would somebody gun down a GI who drove a lousy truck for a battery supply section?

Then he saw the killer turn toward him. The man's expression remained impassive. His eyes were still calm and cool.

"Jesus," Johnson whispered. "I'm next."

The sergeant did not have a gun. But he did have a weapon. The truck. Maybe he could run the bastard over before he blasted bullets through the windshield. As Johnson moved toward the driver's seat, he felt something jar the cab. He turned to see a hand holding a pistol at the open window. The barrel was pointed at his face. A tremendous roar seemed to fill the inside of Staff Sergeant Harlon Johnson's head. It was the last sound he ever heard. A bullet punched through his forehead and tore a ragged exit at the back of his skull. A pink-and-red spray of brains and blood covered the inside of the cab.

"Dummkopf," a man with long dark hair shouted as he approached the truck. "You were not to shoot the *Amerikaner* until he left the truck. Bloody mess."

A tall gaunt figure stepped from the passenger's side of the cab. His mouth was twisted in a sneer and his eyes gazed at the newcomer with amusement. A Luger P.08 pistol was still in his bony fist, smoke curling from its muzzle.

"Herr Werner." The blond gunman spoke to the long-haired man as he walked around the cow and began to unscrew the silencer from the barrel of his Walther PPK. "May I suggest you do not offend Gunther? I know him far better than you. Believe me, you do not want to anger him. *Verstehen Sie?*"

Klaus Werner stared at Gunther, noting the cruel smile and unblinking eyes of the gaunt killer. Werner was tempted to reach for the Czech M1950 pistol in his coat pocket, but he realized he needed his comrades. Besides, Gunther and the blond Rudolf Kortze were ruthless killers who would not hesitate to gun him down if he made any hostile move.

"Ja," Werner said, bobbing his shoulder-length brown hair. "I understand. It's just that now we have to put up with a disgusting mess inside the cab of the truck."

"I'll have Gunther clean it up," Kortze said with a thin smile. "He usually follows orders quite well. Sometimes he smells the blood of a kill only seconds away and he cannot wait."

Werner merely nodded again. He hated these people—Gunther, Kortze and the others. They were not soldiers of the cause, warriors of the people's struggle. No, Kortze and his kind were part of a feared and despised regime that most people, including Werner, would rather forget had ever existed.

Yet circumstances had united Werner and his comrades with the monstrous minions of the old regime, the hated power that had challenged the world almost forty years ago. The regime had been beaten and trampled, but not totally destroyed. Kortze and Gunther were proof of that. Werner hated having such men for allies, but they still shared a common goal.

And like all fanatics, Werner believed the end justifies the means. He felt no revulsion when Gunther dragged the corpse of S. Sgt. Johnson from the cab and dumped it on the ground. Werner glanced down at the bloodied, bullet-shattered face of the American. He felt no remorse. The Americans were the enemy and the enemy must die.

Klaus Werner was not as different from Kortze and Gunther as he liked to think. They all regarded murder to be a simple act of expediency; it was a tool of their political lunacy.

Rudolf Kortze knelt beside Johnson's corpse and searched through his pockets. He smiled when he discovered a pack of American cigarettes. If nothing else, the *Amerikaneren* certainly knew how to make good cigarettes. He helped himself to one of the smokes and lit it with a battered old Krugler lighter. The double Sig runes of the SS were engraved in the nickel-plated lighter. It had once belonged to his father, *Standartenführer* Kortze. Rudolf kept the lighter as a constant reminder of his father's dedication and his own responsibility to duty. He was totally devoted to his father's regime, to a cause that had started long before he had been born.

"All has gone according to plan," Kortze declared as he drew deeply on the cigarette, savoring the smoke.

"True," Werner admitted without enthusiasm. "But we have yet to accomplish our main objective, *kamerad*."

"Twelve days from now, that too will be a reality," Kortze insisted, gazing at the burning end of his cigarette. "Then, no power on the face of the earth will dare defy us."

Klaus Werner nodded in agreement and softly whispered under his breath, "*Sieg heil*, you lunatic."

1

Gary Manning was a runner, but he was not a sprinter. His thickly muscled body was not designed for speed; strength and endurance had always been his forte.

In the crispness of a morning in northern Canada, Manning was jogging through woodland. He seldom kept track of how many miles he ran. On that particular morning, he could not have told anyone if he had covered five miles or fifty. The large man was trying to come to grips with frustration and emotional stress. He was determined to exercise those feelings out of his system.

Even as a child Manning had always attacked any task with dogmatic single-mindedness. When he found a purpose worth his effort he always threw himself—body, mind and spirit— into the breach until he accomplished the job.

This bulldog determination and almost fanatical drive had been both a blessing and a curse. It had made Manning a successful businessman. It had helped him earn commendations during his military career and allowed him to develop the steel nerves and surgeonlike dexterity needed to become one of the Western Hemisphere's leading experts on explosives and demolition.

Yet these same character traits had also isolated him from friends and family. He had lost many friends because he was a man who had little interest in or time for social functions. Manning's workaholic nature had long ago caused his marriage to fall apart. Of his immediate family, only a sister and brother-in-law remained and Manning saw little of them because his duties kept him constantly busy.

Manning's behavior had made him something of a social hermit, but in his line of work, this proved to be an advantage. Since he was a difficult man to become close to, few people knew him well and few cared enough to question his activities. Prying eyes and long noses seldom extended into his business matters or personal life.

If he vanished for a week or two, his associates assumed he had flown off on a business trip, or, maybe he had finally decided to take a long-overdue vacation. No one suspected that Manning might be involved in any type of covert activity.

No one would have guessed that he was a member of Phoenix Force, the most highly trained team of antiterrorist specialists in the world.

Gary Manning's life was crowded with work, duties and responsibilities, but he was still a man. He was not immune to loneliness; he felt

the need to love and be loved. And he grieved
when he lost someone he cared for.

Their last mission had sent Phoenix Force to
northern Africa where they were pitted against a
power-mad psychotic who could have given Idi
Amin lessons in brutality. None of Phoenix
Force's assignments was easy, but the last had
been worse than most. Especially for Manning.

He had fallen in love with a woman named
Nemtala. It had been the first close relationship he had had since his wife Lorraine di-
vorced him. But he had lost Nemtala in a
bloody battle. And the bitterness and pain of
having love cruelly ripped from his heart was
tremendous.

The mission had been a success and all five
members of Phoenix Force had survived. Yet a
part of Gary Manning had been torn from his
soul and buried with Nemtala.

Manning jogged around a fallen tree and continued to trot in his steady machinelike manner
across the grassy floor of the forest. Perspiration streamed down his face and soaked his
baggy, gray sweat suit. Eventually, he felt
muscles straining in protest. Thighs and calves
ached, lungs burned, his breath became ragged.
Still, he pushed himself to keep going. Run her
out of your mind, he thought. Run her out of
your heart. Keep going....

A figure stepped from a cluster of undersized
young pine trees. Gary Manning instantly came
to a dead stop. His legs nearly buckled and he

staggered as he fought to keep his balance. The tall black shape stepped forward.

Manning immediately recognized the man. No one who met the impressive fighting machine in black combat fatigues could ever forget him. Even without the fabled Beretta in a shoulder holster and the big steel .44 AutoMag on his hip, the man known as Colonel John Phoenix, Mack Bolan, the Executioner, could never be mistaken for anyone else.

"You've been a hard man to get in touch with," the big warrior remarked. "We've been tracking you in a helicopter for the last eight miles. You didn't even notice."

Manning nodded in reply, panting too hard to talk. He finally caught his breath. "A little...exercise...never...hurt anyone, Colonel."

Phoenix looked into Manning's face. His cool, dark blue eyes seemed to bore right into the Canadian's brain, sucking out his thoughts.

"Something bothering you, soldier?"

"Nothing I can't handle," Manning assured him.

"Make sure of it." The warrior's voice was hard. "If you're not able to function at peak level, don't even try to. It won't be just your life on the line."

Manning understood. The moment he had seen Colonel Phoenix in the forest, he knew why the Executioner was searching for him.

The colonel stepped forward and handed

Manning a thick manila envelope. The Canadian waited for instructions.

"In a nutshell," the Executioner began, "there's a new wave of terrorism in West Germany."

"German Red Army Faction?" Manning asked. "Or the Baader-Meinhof gang?"

"We don't know what group is responsible for what's happening over there now. All we know for sure is it's damn serious."

"It always is," the Canadian remarked. "But the West German antiterrorist unit can generally handle anything the terrorists throw at them. I served as an adviser for the GSG-Nine courses in explosives and bomb disposal."

"I know," the warrior said, nodding. "Grenzschutzgruppe-Neun is damn good—one of the best antiterrorist outfits in the world. When they're stumped you know the situation is bad. That envelope contains everything we know about the terrorists thus far. It's damn little to go on. Don't be fooled by the thickness of that package. We included the complete 201 files of all the victims of the terrorists' activities, along with any other information we could get about them."

"Two-oh-one files?" Manning raised his eyebrows. "U.S. military personnel?"

"That's right," Phoenix confirmed. "And except for the fact all the victims were in the United States Army stationed in the republic of Germany, they seem to have nothing in common. No link to suggest they were connected in any way.''

"Except death," the Canadian mused grimly.

"Yeah," the Executioner agreed. "It looks like somebody has declared open season on American servicemen in USAEUR."

"And you want us to cancel their hunting license."

"Permanently," the colonel said firmly. "You can read through the file in the chopper. We'll fly you back to your cabin."

Phoenix turned and marched into the forest. Manning followed.

"You'll be working with Army Intelligence and GSG-Nine," Phoenix explained, "so there won't be any problem transporting weapons and equipment to Europe. No hassle from the customs people. You won't have to take too much since GSG-Nine will supply you with anything you might need."

"What about transportation?"

"Army Air Corps will fly you directly to Frankfurt, Germany. The others will meet you there."

"They've already been contacted?"

The Executioner nodded. "They've received messages in the usual manner. They'll be fully briefed when they get to Germany. The Intel boys tend to be close-mouthed with everybody. Even their own people. They've been told not only to cooperate with you guys, but to take orders from you as well. Naturally, they don't know anything about Phoenix Force, but they've been informed that you five are the best in the business and you've been sent directly by order of the president.''

"Shouldn't be any flak,"Manning said hopefully.

"Better not be," Phoenix commented. "McCarter is probably in Germany by now. Katz and Ohara should be on their way by now and Encizo flew out of the Miami International Airport about an hour ago.''

They walked to a clearing in the woods. A Bell Huey helicopter waited for the pair. The pilot started the engine and the big propeller began to rotate.

"You're quite a tracker," the Canadian stated. "You found me out here.''

"If we had been enemies, I could have killed you," the Executioner said. "Remember the survivalist game, Gary?''

"I know," Manning agreed grimly. "I was careless today.''

"Something is eating your insides like an emotional cancer," Phoenix insisted. "One more time, soldier: are you sure you've got your stuff together? I'm not going to send you to Germany if your head—or your *heart*—is somewhere else. Too many lives are at stake to allow you to get careless again.''

Manning met the colonel's hard gaze. "You've given me the assignment. I can handle it.''

Mack Bolan smiled with satisfaction. He knew fighting men. He could evaluate them. Whatever emotional turmoil Manning had to cope with, it would not interfere with the mission. Manning was ready again. Combat ready.

2

General Karl Lieter stood at the head of the walnut conference table and addressed the men gathered for the top-secret meeting at the BND headquarters in Bonn. The Bundesnachrichtendienst is the federal intelligence service of West Germany. With the Communist nations of Eastern Europe at her borders, the Federal Republic of Germany needs a damn good intel organization. The BND is one of the best.

"Perhaps we should start with introductions," Lieter declared in excellent English that barely contained a trace of accent.

"Colonel Matthew Arness," a tall, broad-shouldered figure clad in a dress-green U.S. Army uniform, announced. "United States Army Intelligence, USAEUR Sector."

"Colonel Theodore O'Connor," the other U.S. Army officer stated. O'Connor was a head shorter than Arness. His dark hair was streaked with silver and his thick bushy eyebrows gave him an owllike appearance. "USAEUR NATO Security Forces."

O'Connor seemed to resent having to state his occupation to a roomful of strangers. Especially since most of them were not Americans.

"I am Colonel Ludwig Bohler," a muscular blond German National declared. "Grenzschutzgruppe-neun."

"You chaps must have quite an organization," David McCarter remarked. The handsome fox-faced Englishman displayed a boyish grin. "Simply pronouncing it is an impressive task."

"We generally call it GSG-Nine," Bohler smiled in return.

He glanced across the table at the senior member of Phoenix Force. Colonel Yakov Katzenelenbogen rolled his eyes at the ceiling. *God of our fathers,* the Israeli thought. *Why does McCarter continue to make ridiculous remarks? Will he never learn the value and virtues of tact?*

McCarter was a highly trained professional antiterrorist. A veteran of Great Britain's Strategic Air Service, he was a superb pilot, a former national champion of the British Pistol Marksmanship Team and an expert in almost every form of combat. Even before he had been recruited for Phoenix Force, McCarter had impressive experience as an antiterrorist and a fighting man. He had seen action in Southeast Asia, spent two years in the British colony of Hong Kong on special assignment against Communist subversives, and he had been part of the SAS team that hit the Iranian embassy in London.

David McCarter was a lion in combat, but he tended to be short-tempered and high-strung when he was not on the battlefield. The Briton lived for adventure and action. Katzenelenbogen suspected McCarter would die of boredom if he could not get into a fight every six months. McCarter needed an outlet. He had devoted his life to acquiring skills useful only in combat. If he could not exercise this expertise, he felt he was wasting his time and that made him surly and abrasive.

Colonel O'Connor glared at McCarter. Slowly he eyeballed the other members of Phoenix Force. Gary Manning sat as still as a statue. Rafael Encizo, a dark handsome Cuban who looked ten years younger than his forty-plus years, appeared bored by the conference. Keio Ohara, a tall Japanese who dressed like a model for *Esquire*, read over a file folder. Probably doesn't understand it, O'Connor thought sourly.

The NATO Security man looked at Yakov and shook his head. The Israeli resembled a college professor. He was at least ten pounds overweight and he had to be in his midfifties. Worse, his right arm had been amputated at the elbow, the empty sleeve pinned back to the stump. Jesus, O'Connor thought, these men are supposed to be crack antiterrorists.

"I want to know exactly who you men are," O'Connor demanded. "*What* are you? CIA?"

"Knights Templar," David McCarter replied with a sneer. He had noticed O'Connor's disapproving glance at Katz. The Briton decided he was not going to like O'Connor very much and he damn well wanted the bloody snob to know it.

"Let's not be rude," Katz urged McCarter, as he fired a Camel cigarette with a battered Ronson lighter.

"If we're going to cooperate with you people..." O'Connor began angrily.

"You want us to be CIA?" Rafael Encizo shrugged. "Okay. You can think that if it'll make you happy, Colonel. But you know our authority comes from the Oval Office. Don't try to pull rank on us. You'll lose."

O'Connor glared at Encizo. The Cuban met his gaze squarely. Rafael Encizo did not frighten easily. He had been to hell and back. A veteran of the Bay of Pigs invasion, Encizo had been a political prisoner at Castro's Isle of Pines. He had been beaten and tortured, but never broken.

An expert frogman and knife fighter, the Cuban was a part-time security investigator and full-time warrior. O'Connor did not look into Encizo's hard dark eyes for long.

"Colonel O'Connor," Ludwig Bohler said, sighing, "these men are here to help us. I can personally vouch for the ability of Lieutenant Manning. He was an instructor for GSG-Nine back in 1973. Herr Manning is the finest demolitions expert I have ever met. He is also one of the best rifle marksmen in the world. We should be thankful for his aid in this matter."

"Thank you, Colonel." Manning nodded. "And may I say that my fellow team members are as qualified in their fields as I am. . . if not more so. They're the best in the world."

"I have no doubt." Bohler smiled. "Colonel Katz could probably teach us all a thing or two about dealing with terrorists, eh?"

The other men present—including the Israeli's fellow Phoenix Force members—turned to stare at Katz.

"Ludwig. . . Colonel Bohler and I did a little work together back in 1974," he explained. "A splinter group from the PLO was trying to reorganize the Second June Movement. I was still with Mossad at the time. They sent me to try to track down the Arab terrorists before they could team up with their German counterparts. That's how Ludwig and I met."

"Indeed." Bohler nodded. "And we worked well together, too."

"The hardest part was surviving the celebration after the work was finished," the Israeli laughed. "My head still hurts when I think of that hangover. Are you certain we were drinking schnapps and not some sort of rocket fuel?"

Keio Ohara, the only member of Phoenix Force who had yet to speak, cleared his throat before breaking the silence.

"Could we discuss some of the details concerning this terrorist activity?" he asked. "I'm afraid my information is rather sketchy."

"Right you are, Keio," McCarter agreed.

"All I bloody got was a telegram telling me to get my arse to Frankfurt and to wait for the rest of you misfits to join me."

"That's about all I got too," Encizo added.

"Colonel Arness probably knows the most about the details of recent events," Karl Lieter said.

"I wish we had something useful to tell you," the Army Intel officer sighed.

"Just tell us what you know," Manning suggested.

"Three months ago, an Army jeep with two passengers—a duty driver and a second lieutenant—vanished somewhere between Pinder Barracks and Fürth. The soldiers were later found outside Zirndorf. Both were shot and stripped down to their skivvies. We still haven't found any clues to suggest who did it or why.

"Two weeks later, a supply truck heading back to Merrill Barracks with some office equipment and TA-Fifty disappeared. The supply sergeant and driver were found about six kilometers from Nürnberg. They'd also been shot."

"Tell them what happened last month," O'Connor impatiently demanded.

Arness cast a perturbed glance at O'Connor before he continued. "An MP jeep with two military policemen detailed to guard a NATO site failed to report to their station. They too were found murdered."

"Uniforms missing?" Encizo inquired, looking for a pattern.

"Yes," Arness confirmed. "The area where they were murdered is only a quarter of a mile from the NATO site. No one heard the shots that killed the men."

"Silencers," Gary Manning remarked. "Pass me the ballistics reports on the slugs taken out of the victims."

"We'll all want to go over the reports in further detail," McCarter added. "Anything might contain a clue to this business. Never know until you look."

"Of course," Arness agreed, adjusting the straps of a shoulder holster containing a .45 caliber M1911A1 autoloader. "Most of us have taken to carrying a gun lately."

"That's nice for you officers," Encizo commented. "But most of the victims have been enlisted men and I bet you haven't allowed them to carry arms."

"How do you think our German hosts would react if they saw American servicemen trotting about the streets with guns?" Colonel O'Connor snapped. "They'd think we were still occupational forces in their country."

"Are you more concerned about appearances or lives, Colonel?" the Cuban asked.

"Excuse me," Ohara broke in. "In every case you've mentioned, Colonel Arness, a vehicle was involved. Have any of these trucks or jeeps been recovered?"

"No," Arness replied.

The Army Intel officer gazed at the Japanese with interest. Arness had been stationed in Okinawa, Korea and Vietnam, but he could not recall having encountered an Oriental as tall as Ohara. Keio was over six feet—taller than McCarter.

Height seemed to be the only thing McCarter and Ohara had in common. The Briton was quick to speak, occasionally rash and sharp-tongued. The Japanese, however, listened and evaluated information before he spoke. Ohara was neatly dressed in a single-breasted dark blue suit, a striped shirt and a burgundy tie. McCarter's sport jacket looked as if he had used it as a knapsack before he put it on.

"It seems unlikely that someone would go to such trouble just to obtain the vehicles," Katz commented.

"That's not all that was taken," Encizo added. "Don't forget the uniforms."

Colonel O'Connor snorted. "One can go to any pawnshop in Germany and buy practically any article of U.S. military apparel from combat boots to MP leather belts and holsters."

"But the uniforms were still taken," the Cuban insisted. "I still think that might be important. Why else did the killers do it every time?"

"Taking the uniforms, ID cards and dog tags would make it a bit more difficult to identify the bodies," McCarter said. "They might have done it to buy a little extra time."

"But who are *they*?" Katz mused. "Do any of you have any idea?"

"Of course we've been looking into that," General Lieter answered. "We don't have anything solid, but naturally we have to put the German Red Army Faction and the Baader-Meinhof gang at the head of the suspect list."

"But weren't the leaders of Baader-Meinhof wiped out?" McCarter asked.

"A few of them are still in prison," Bohler said. "That's only because we don't have capital punishment in Germany—*yet*. The gang's founders, Andreas Baader and Ulrike Meinhof did us a favor and committed suicide. Unfortunately, they left at least one successor to take command of the gang."

"Brigitte Mohnhaupt," Gary Manning supplied. "Baader selected her for the job back in 1977 when she was still serving time in Stammham prison."

"Yes," Katz said grimly. "They sent her to South Yemen where she received extensive training from the Soviets and Cubans who run the terrorist schools there. Mohnhaupt was a true professional by the time she masterminded the attempt to assassinate General Kroezer."

"That's true," Bohler admitted. "But the remnants of the old Baader-Meinhof gang and most of the Second June Movement are behind bars or they've teamed up with the Red Army Faction. The RAF is the largest and most dangerous terrorist organization in Germany today.''

"But not all terrorist activity in Germany is committed by Germans," Lieter hastily added. "A good deal of it involves Italians, Arabs and Turks. We have a very large Turkish population here.''

"The Turkish Gray Wolves seem to have quite a following in Germany," Katz commented. "Mehmet Ali Agca received assistance from the Gray Wolves here after he fled Turkey. Of course, it was the Bulgarians who transported Agca to Italy where he tried to assassinate Pope John Paul.''

"If you want to confuse matters we might as well include the Italian Red Brigades, the Corsican Liberation Front, the Irish Republican Army," O'Connor growled. "Need I go on?"

"If it will make you happy," McCarter muttered.

"When an act of terrorism occurs," Encizo began, "various terrorist groups are usually falling all over each other trying to claim credit, even if they didn't do it. But that hasn't happened this time, has it?''

"No," Arness said. "We've tried to keep a lid on this. Getting multiple crank calls would only confuse the investigation. But it is strange that they haven't contacted us.''

"This is odd," Gary Manning said after reading the ballistics reports. "The bullets used by the killers were from a 7.65mm Mauser HSC, a

Walther PPK in 9mm *kurtz*—same as .380 caliber—and two Luger pistols. One was 9mm and the other was 7.65."

"So what?" Encizo said. "They're all German-made firearms."

"That's my point," the Canadian explained. "Most European terrorists, regardless of nationality, get their weapons from the Communists—usually Czech machine pistols and Soviet automatic rifles, grenades and pistols. What the hell are these murderers doing with a 7.65 Luger? It's a goddamn museum piece."

"What difference does that make?" O'Connor demanded. "What I want to know is what you people intend to do about it? I've got a lot of responsibility to the NATO Defense Forces here. The murder of those two MPs proves our security may be in jeopardy."

"Perhaps we'll be better able to decide what should be done if we know what actions have already been taken," said Ohara, at twenty-nine the youngest member of Phoenix Force.

"Since a direct threat to national security has yet to be established," General Lieter said, "this matter does not technically fall under the jurisdiction of the BND. However, we'll do whatever we can to assist you."

"GSG-Nine is doing everything possible to get a lead on the identity and whereabouts of the terrorists," Colonel Bohler said. "Right now, we're concentrating on suspected members of terrorist organizations, especially suspected members of the Red Army Faction. We're hoping one of them will lead us to the terrorists' lair.''

"What about the U.S. military?'' Katz asked Colonel Arness.

"We're conducting an investigation, of course," Colonel Arness said. "But we haven't had much success. To be honest, right now we're concentrating on prevention.''

"Well, all NATO can do at this time is reinforce security until the crisis is over," O'Connor said defensively.

"What sort of precautions, Colonel Arness?'' Keio asked.

"Well,'' the intelligence officer sighed, "not much. Memos to personnel to increase security. Guards have been doubled and issued ammunition. . . .''

"What?'' Encizo raised his eyebrows. "You mean to say sentries at U.S. military bases generally stand guard with *empty* weapons?''

"Usually," Arness said, squirming. "There have been a few firearm accidents in the past, and pressures from upstairs made us restrict the issuing of ammo to troops under most circumstances. . . .''

The Cuban shook his head. Gary Manning picked up the conversation.

"In short, the precautions taken are much the same as they were in the seventies during the Baader-Meinhof and Black September incidents?''

"With one addition," Arness said. "Since most of the incidents have occurred near bases in Bavaria, we've urged post commanders to send an armed guard with any vehicle that leaves the base."

"What kind of guard?" David McCarter asked as he approached the table. "What are they armed with?"

"Most are MPs armed with .45-caliber pistols," Arness answered, watching the Englishman place an aluminum suitcase on the table.

"That's not good enough," McCarter declared as he worked the case's combination locks. "Not when you're dealing with terrorists. Back in the SAS, I learned that you have to have enough firepower to make a good impression on those bastards."

He opened the case and extracted an Ingram Model 10 machine pistol. The compact boxlike gun, with a stubby barrel and a wire stock, is an excellent close-quarters weapon. Although it can be fired semiauto, on full automatic it blasts out nine-millimeter rounds at 1200 rounds per minute.

"You need something like this," McCarter continued, shoving a 32-round magazine into the well at the pistol grips of the M-10. "This baby will get your point across, believe me."

No one in the room could argue with that.

3

Heinrich Müller sat in his armchair behind his thick metal desk and stared at the flag mounted on the wall. Although fifty-two years old, Müller had retained a slender muscled physique that would do justice to a man twenty years his junior. His tanned skin had begun to look leathery from too many summers spent in Brazil. Wrinkles and silver-gray hair were all that betrayed his age.

"You have no idea what those days were like, my friends," Müller began, gazing at the black swastika within a great white circle in the center of the red flag.

"I was only a boy when it started," he continued. "Too young to fully appreciate the glory the Reich had brought to Germany. Unity, purpose and power. They were ours in those days."

Helga Konner, only half listening to Müller, glanced at her husband, but Norbert's expression remained impassive, expressing no feeling. A stoop-shouldered man, barely thirty-years old, Norbert Konner wore thick glasses and a small black goatee. He looked like a cross between an owl and a goat.

Konner and his stocky blond wife resembled a pair of schoolteachers more than professional terrorists. Since their politics were rooted in Marxist-Leninism, they had little use for Müller's reminiscing over the "glories" of Nazi Germany.

"Of course," Müller continued, "I learned what it all meant. I was a member of the Hitler Youth Movement, and I was educated that we were to be the Master Race, ruling all of Europe if not the entire world. We tried to rid the world of the Jews, the Slavs and the other barbarians. We were called butchers, but we were only trying to save our society from the elements that would destroy it...."

Müller's eyes misted over. "I was only seventeen when I received the rank of *Leutnant* in the SS with a squad of brave young soldiers under my command. We were to inherit the world. It was our destiny."

The Nazi shook his head sadly. "That was the dream, but reality fell from the skies when British, Americans and Russians bombed our cities, defeated our armies. The Russians, those savages, plundered, raped and killed German civilians."

He glared at the Konners. "You should have seen how they forced themselves on German girls and tore them apart with their bayonets when they were through. Perhaps then you would not boast of your loyalty to communism. Did you know Stalin's regime executed approximately thirty million Soviet citizens? Compare that with the alleged six million killed by Hitler's Final Solution. Tell me, Herr Konner, is your devil any better than mine?''

"We have no love for the Soviets, Herr Müller," Norbert declared. "My wife and I did not join the Baader-Meinhof gang because we wanted to help the Russians. My comrades and I believed we could unite Germany under a single Marxist government. We were foolish to believe the Soviets gave us arms and assistance and expected nothing in return. We were not revolutionaries; we were cannon fodder, used by the Russian KGB to disrupt the Federal Republic of Germany. The main goal behind Soviet-influenced terrorism is to make a country more repressive. The host country is supposed to overreact to the violence of the rebels and force more restrictions on the entire population. Then the masses will support the *real* revolution, which will also be inspired by the Soviet puppet masters in Moscow."

"My husband and I also despise the Soviet Stalinists," Helga said. "Like you, we want Germany to be a strong united country, an example to true revolutionaries throughout the world."

"Revolution?" Müller scoffed. "When you contacted ODESSA you spoke not of global revolts for your idiot working class, but of Germany for Germans. The Organisation der ehemaligen SS Angehörigen consists largely of old men, weary German warriors who are tired of running and hiding from the Israeli death squads and other Nazi hunters. ODESSA consists of men like me who have been forced to spend most of their lives in Paraguay, Brazil or some other foreign hellhole, hoping that one day we would be able to return to Germany to live the rest of our lives in our own country.

"And it is fortunate that ODESSA also consists of our sons," Müller said fiercely, "proud young advocates of national socialism. They will risk their lives for Germany. Although born in a dozen other countries, they know Germany is their homeland. It is theirs by virtue of their Aryan blood and the sacrifices of their fathers. They are warrior stock, fighting men. That is where we differ from you former Baader-Meinhof members—we are leaders, but you have never been able to function without the help of the Soviets. That is why you need us so desperately."

Helga's face reddened with anger, but Norbert spoke before she could voice her opinion. "A united Germany is our common goal, Herr Müller. We should not argue so among ourselves. The Americans and their puppet government of German capitalists in the West are as much our enemy as the Russians and their followers in the east. These are our enemies, *not* each other."

Müller shrugged and opened a desk drawer. He extracted a 9mm Luger pistol. He had carried the gun most of his life and handled it as one might a sacred religious object. The Nazi began to fieldstrip his pistol.

"You are right, Norbert," Müller agreed. "I am sorry that I spoke so harshly, but we have suffered greatly over many long years. We grow impatient as the time of conquest and victory approaches. Of course, if ODESSA did not trust you, we would not have agreed to join you in this venture. We have been inactive for the past thirty-seven years because we have had to concentrate on simply surviving while we planned for the future. When one must hide in a stinking South American jungle for almost four decades, there seems little hope for a future. Fortunately, we had finances and resources that helped protect us and allowed us to support this new noble war against Germany's oppressors."

Ja, Helga thought bitterly. The SS and the Gestapo had stolen huge sums of currency from every nation they occupied during the war. They seized diamonds, gold, priceless art objects and other valuables. They sacked French museums and Polish jewelry stores and ripped gold teeth from the mouths of Jewish prisoners in their death camps.

No one could fault the Nazis for not preparing for a rainy day. They put the bulk of their ill-gotten gains into Swiss bank accounts under assumed names. The ODESSA nest egg had continued to grow. Almost forty years later, they had a fortune worth billions.

Müller smiled coldly at the Konners. "ODESSA plans a major operation for years. We study, evaluate and act with the greatest of care. Quite different from what you're used to. The Baader-Meinhof gang never planned anything more complex than a simple bank robbery. You spent too much time reading Karl Marx instead of developing strategy...."

Norbert Konner had heard enough. He suddenly rose from his chair and slapped both palms on the top of Müller's desk. He glared into the face of the Nazi, meeting Müller's icy gray eyes with his own steady gaze.

"What you've said is true," Konner admitted in a hard voice. "But it is also true that *we*—Helga and I—conceived this operation. What would you have done without us?"

Müller's jaw muscles tensed, but he remained silent as Konner continued.

"Our experience with the Baader-Meinhof gang taught us how to avoid the German authorities. I'm talking about the police and the BND that are here *today*, in the present. Not your storm troopers and Gestapo of the past. We know the reality of modern Germany. We helped your people get into the country through our connections with the international terrorist networks. We got you this old toy factory to use as a headquarters, set up right under the noses of the authorities, yet perfectly secure.

"And, *we* were the ones who found out the details about the American installations. You

and the rest of the ODESSA elite are anach-
ronisms and your 'brave Aryan sons of the
Reich' are foreigners who know as much about
Germany as I know about the North Pole. You
sent your offspring to learn about nuclear
weaponry, and they learned well. But where
would you and your whiz kids be without us?
You'd be in Brazil remembering the regime of a
madman."

Helga was stunned by her husband's out-
burst. She did not like dealing with the Nazis.
Slowly she opened her purse and reached inside
for an H&K .380 automatic. There were at least
a dozen storm troopers stationed at the factory,
and Müller kept an MP-40 machine pistol under
his desk. Her little pistol would be no match
against such odds, yet it was better than
nothing.

The tension in the room broke abruptly when
Müller tilted his head back and laughed.

"Ah, my dear Norbert," he exclaimed with
delight. "You are not the spineless intellectual
you appear to be. You have stood up for your
people and your role in this matter. You are
right, of course. ODESSA and your people need
each other if we are to succeed. You are also
right about *der Führer*."

The Konners stared at Müller. He laughed
even harder at their expressions of astonishment.

"Of course we realized Hitler was insane,"
Müller told them. "Why do you think so many

of us planned our escapes so well in advance. It was well-known that Hitler was dying. Some said it was a brain tumor, but I suspect he was suffering from advanced syphilis. There was talk of replacing *der Führer* with Himmler and Bormann. That would have been interesting, since they hated each other.

"Yet let us not forget Hitler's accomplishments. He helped unite Germany under the banner of national socialism and he brought our country out of economic ruin and made her a strong and feared nation. Just as we will make Germany a powerful single country once more, independent of the capitalist West and the Communist East."

The Konners sighed with relief. Müller clasped his hands together and smiled slyly at his guests.

"Now," he said, "Helga, please leave your pistol in your purse. After all, friends should not shoot each other, *ja*?"

4

Rafael Encizo yawned. He pulled the olive baseball cap from his head and glanced at the sergeant's stripes tacked above the brim. Encizo wondered if he would be able to find enough time to get acquainted with a fraülein or two before they left Germany. The Cuban loved women—beautiful, charming women.

Then the deuce and a half ton truck bounced as it ran over a rock in the road. Encizo's mind was jarred back to the mission at hand.

"Shit," the driver muttered. "Sorry about that. I didn't see it in time."

"I don't imagine this road is traveled much," Encizo commented as he gazed at the dark evergreens that flanked both sides of the road.

"Not until recently," Sergeant First Class Tim Bently, the driver, said.

A wiry, lean-faced man who appeared younger than his thirty-two years, Bently wore the rank of specialist fifth class to avoid suspicion about why a senior NCO was driving a truck. Bently was a member of Army Intelligence, and a Vietnam combat veteran who knew how to use the .45-caliber Colt 1911 A1 that hung in a special holster under his seat.

"Figure this is a wild-goose chase?" Bently inquired, glancing at the forest as if he expected the trees to attack at any moment.

"Could be," Encizo shrugged. "All we know about the terrorists is they tend to attack lone military vehicles in remote areas. Maybe we'll get lucky and lure them out."

Maybe, the Cuban thought sourly. He and the other members of Phoenix Force had been riding back and forth in Army jeeps and trucks for three days, favoring the most tranquil and least traveled roads between different U.S. military installations. So far, the terrorists had not snapped at the bait.

"How do you like the ride so far?" Encizo called cheerfully to McCarter, who was hidden in the back of the deuce and a half.

"It's a bloody roller coaster back here," the Briton complained. "Do you two think it's fun to run into potholes or something?"

"Sure," the Cuban replied. "It's sort of like getting a massage while you ride. Have you contacted Yakov yet?"

"Just about to," McCarter growled. "Be patient."

In the back of the truck, McCarter sat on the floor, surrounded by wooden crates that supplied concealment and could serve as cover in a firefight. Dressed in black camouflage fatigues and beret, he wore a Browning Hi-Power 9mm autoloader in a shoulder holster and a web belt complete with hand grenades and spare magazine pouches. McCarter also had his Ingram M-10 close at hand.

He picked up a walkie-talkie and pressed its button. "Foxhound One, this is Foxhound Two. Over."

"Foxhound Two, this is Foxhound One," Yakov Katzenelenbogen replied. "We read you loud and clear. Over."

The Israeli was disguised as a U.S. Army colonel being chauffeured around remote Bavarian roads a few miles away in a jeep driven by another Army Intel agent.

"Nothing going on at this end, mate," McCarter stated. "Over."

"Same here." Katz sounded as disappointed as McCarter felt.

"Did you contact Foxhound Three yet? Over," Katz inquired.

"Negative," McCarter replied. "Over."

Foxhound Three was Gary Manning and Keio Ohara. Disguised in the same manner as Encizo and McCarter, they were riding in another truck, with the Canadian playing sergeant in the cab and the Japanese hidden in the back of the rig.

"Don't bother," Katz said. "I got a call from them less than a minute ago. Nothing going on there either. Over."

"Over and out, you old fox," McCarter said.

"Oh-oh," Bently muttered as he turned a bend in the road and discovered a large beer truck blocking their path. "This could be it."

Encizo noticed the soldier's calm response to possible danger and mentally commended Colonel Arness for selecting Bently.

The beer truck's back gate lay on the ground and a dozen wooden kegs were scattered around. A big, potbellied man clad in overalls and a cap was rolling one of the barrels toward the truck.

"Don't jump to conclusions, Sarge," the Cuban urged, unzipping his field jacket in case he had to draw a Smith & Wesson .38 snubnose from a holster on his hip.

The Cuban glanced at the AWOL bag between his feet. The wire stock of an M-10 machine pistol jutted from the opening.

"Was ist los," the fat man greeted in the traditional Bavarian manner.

"Grüß Gott," Bently replied in German. "Had an accident, *mein herr*?"

"Ja," the Bavarian said as he approached the deuce and a half. "The back door went kaput and my beer fell out everywhere. Can you help me load it back on?"

Encizo noticed the fat man had slipped a hand into a pocket of his overalls. Bently also saw this and reached for the .45 Colt under his seat.

At the same instant, McCarter spotted a pair of men creeping from the forest near the rear of the truck. Both carried pistols with sound suppressors attached to the barrels. The Briton immediately grabbed his M-10 and thrust the stubby barrel at the pair.

"Raisen sie hands," he shouted, forgetting the correct German words in his excitement.

The gunmen responded by raising their weapons and taking aim at the deuce and a half. McCarter's Ingram spit a furious volley of 9mm destruction at the pair, cutting them down before either man could squeeze a trigger.

As the metallic chatter of the machine pistol erupted the fat German yanked a diminutive .25-caliber Bauer automatic from his pocket. The roar of Bently's .45 instantly replied to the threat. The German screamed and staggered backward with a heavy 230-grain slug in the center of his flabby chest. Bently fired another round into the man. The would-be ambusher crashed to the ground in an obscene twitching heap.

Rafael Encizo had already pulled his M-10 from the AWOL bag and popped open the passenger's door. He slipped out of the deuce and a half, his attention centered on the beer truck, although he also scanned the trees for more aggressors.

"McCarter?" he shouted, concerned about his partner.

"Two down," McCarter replied. "Any more players at your end?"

As if responding to the Briton's question, an

automatic weapon snarled from a sniper hidden on the opposite side of the beer truck. Nine-millimeter projectiles punched into the windshield of the deuce and a half, reducing it to a network of glass spiderwebbing. Sfc Bently had managed to bail out of the cab in time to avoid the deadly salvo. He swung his .45 at the hidden gunman.

Suddenly, another full-auto weapon erupted from the forest. Encizo saw a long orange tongue of flame jet from the tree line. He heard Bently scream, but did not allow the sound to distract him as he aimed his Ingram at the ambusher and opened fire.

A burst of M-10 slugs splintered bark from a tree trunk, snapped two branches and ripped into the upper torso of the terrorist. The man howled in agony. He stumbled, lost his balance and tumbled onto the road. An old Schmeisser MP-40 submachine gun fell from the wounded man's trembling hands.

Encizo glanced at the fallen body of Sfc Tim Bently. The soldier lay sprawled on his back, his chest pulverized by 9mm slugs. The Cuban turned to face the wounded terrorist. The German hitman was reaching for his fallen weapon. The Cuban stroked the trigger and fired a 3-round burst that split the killer's face and kicked out the back of his skull in a glob of bone, brains and blood.

The machine gunner still stationed at the beer truck fired another volley at Encizo, but the

Cuban was protected by the deuce and a half. McCarter had left his position in the back of the Army truck and crept toward the enemy vehicle.

He caught a glimpse of the big-shouldered, hard-faced gunman at the beer truck. The terrorist was almost seventy-five yards away, a long distance to ask accuracy of an M-10. McCarter fired anyway, attempting to flush the bastard into the open or draw the man's fire, hopefully giving Encizo a better target.

Bullets whined and ricocheted off the metal hood of the beer-truck cab. One stray slug earned a cry of pain from the terrorist. Another MP-40 machine gun flew from numbed fingers and fell to the ground. The gunman whirled away from the cab, his left hand clutching his bullet-torn right biceps. McCarter squeezed the trigger of his Ingram again, only to discover he had exhausted its ammunition.

"Bloody hell," he spit, clawing at a magazine pouch on his belt.

The wounded man quickly yanked open the door of the cab and leaped inside the beer truck. The engine roared to life. Both Encizo and McCarter broke cover and ran toward the enemy vehicle. The Cuban considered shooting at the truck's tires, but decided against it. The truck could still get away if the driver was determined enough. The terrorist could wear a flat tire down to the rim if he had to.

"Cover me," he shouted as he threw his machine pistol to McCarter.

"Jesus," the Englishman muttered, barely catching the Ingram.

Rafael Encizo dashed toward the beer truck as the driver changed gears and stomped on the gas pedal. The vehicle lurched forward violently. Encizo leaped after it, landing on the edge of the open platform.

He tumbled forward in a shoulder roll to absorb the shock of falling on a fast-moving object.

The truck hurtled down the road, stirring up a screen of flying dust.

Encizo hauled himself upright, relieved to discover he had not injured himself. Wondering if he should see a shrink if he survived, the Cuban took a deep breath and began to climb over the wooden slats of the truck frame.

He tried not to think about the risk he was taking or that the driver might see him in a rear-view mirror and steer the truck into the low-hanging branches of trees that seemed to form a murderous blur around him.

Encizo moved to the driver's side, unsheathed his S&W Airweight revolver and swung down the side of the cab. He landed on the running board as he clung to the stem of the mirror and thrust the barrel of his gun into the open window. The driver stared into the black muzzle of the snubnose.

"Stop the truck," Encizo demanded, clinging to the cab tightly and praying that a sudden halt would not throw him off.

But the terrorist responded by stomping on the gas even harder.

Encizo blasted the bastard into oblivion.

The corpse fell to the right, hands still locked on the steering wheel in a death grip. The truck rolled off the road and plunged toward the tree line. Encizo dropped the revolver on the German's convulsing body, seized the wheel and turned it in time to swing the vehicle back onto the road.

Fortunately for Rafael, the truck was headed toward a hill. The incline and the lack of pressure on the gas pedal caused the vehicle to gradually slow down. Sweat poured from Encizo's face as he continued to fight the wheel to avoid crashing into trees.

Finally the truck slowed enough to allow him to yank open the door and slide behind the wheel. Encizo shoved the corpse aside and stomped on the brake. The big machine came to an abrupt halt and trembled as the Cuban shoved the gear into park.

"I've got to quit doing things like this," he gasped, switching off the ignition.

5

The intelligence section of the 544th Artillery Division at Lotton Barracks was located in the basement of a stone building. The fifty-year-old structure had been reinforced with fresh concrete and steel rods.

No one with less than a top-secret clearance was permitted into the intelligence section, and a bazooka would have been required to blast through its steel door. Inside this minifortress, Phoenix Force met with Colonel Arness and Colonel O'Connor in a soundproof conference room.

Yakov Katzenelenbogen, still dressed in a U.S. Army colonel's uniform with silver eagles on his collar, inserted a cigarette into a three-prong steel hook at the end of his right "arm" and fired it.

"I'm sorry about Sergeant Bently," Katz said.

"Your man died bravely, Colonel," Keio Ohara told Arness.

"Tell that to Bently's widow," O'Connor snapped.

"The sergeant knew the risks involved,"

Gary Manning said as he perused a chart featuring drawings and data about various weapons and uniforms of Soviet and East European military forces. "And he volunteered for the job."

"What's your problem, O'Connor?" Rafael Encizo asked bluntly. "Bently was one of Colonel Arness's men. He isn't whining about what happened because he understands that there are casualties in warfare. You know what war is, O'Connor? Or did you spend your time in Nam sitting in an air-conditioned office in Saigon?"

The NATO Security officer slammed his fist on the conference table. "You people conjured up the plan to bait the terrorists, so you're responsible for this. And all you've accomplished so far has been to get another American soldier killed."

David McCarter, who paced the red carpet, a bottle of Coca-Cola in his hand, spun around to attack O'Connor with his razor tongue.

"We also killed five of the enemy, you pompous arse," the Briton said. "Until now, all the casualties were on our side. *Your* side, right? So just shut your mouth unless you can think of something intelligent to say."

"Easy, David," Katz urged. The Israeli glared at O'Connor. "But my friend has a point, Colonel."

"Very well, gentlemen," Arness sighed. "We're on the scoreboard with five dead terrorists. That's satisfying, but it doesn't solve our problem.''

"That's right," O'Connor agreed, hoping he had an ally. "And we know no more about the terrorists than we did before.''

"Not true, Colonel," Manning stated, as he poured himself a cup of coffee. "The BND did a check on the dead men and they came up with some information.''

The Canadian popped open a briefcase on the table and extracted a folder that contained computer printouts, photographs and thumbprints.

"Four of the dead men haven't been identified yet," Manning explained. "Interpol has been contacted and they're checking fingerprint and dental records now. The fifth man has been positively identified as Fredrick Gudagust, a member of the Baader-Meinhof gang. There has been an arrest warrant out for Gudagust in three countries since 1973.''

"Baader-Meinhof," Arness commented. "That means he's probably with the German Red Army Faction now. Figured it must be those bastards.''

"And you're probably right," Encizo said, "but the Red Army Faction usually carry Communist-made weapons—Soviet and Czech guns for the most part. Why were two of the terrorists armed with World War II Nazi submachine guns?''

"Yeah," Manning agreed, glancing over the BND reports. "Another guy had an old Walther

P-38 and another one was packing a Hungarian Model-37 7.65mm pistol that was manufactured when the Nazis occupied the country.''

O'Connor rolled his eyes in exasperation. ''What's your point? The terrorists must have come across an old cache of Nazi weaponry. What difference does that make?''

''None,'' Katz stated. ''*If* that's what happened.''

Damn Israeli is going to give us a lecture about the Holocaust next, O'Connor thought sourly. But he said, ''What is this crap? The Red Army Faction is behind this. Are you soft on Commies or something?''

''Hardly,'' Ohara said. ''We just want to be certain about all the facts before we make any conclusions.''

''Maybe we'd have some answers if we'd been able to take one of the sons of bitches alive,'' McCarter muttered.

''I tried,'' the Cuban sighed, ''but that *cabron* in the beer truck didn't leave me any choice.''

''Have the German authorities checked the truck's license plate?'' Ohara inquired.

''The vehicle was reported stolen from a brewery near Nürnberg four days ago,'' Manning replied.

''Well, if we try any more baiting with these characters we'd better be ready for some real trouble,'' Encizo remarked. ''They had a pretty nasty ambush set up last time. Two machine gunners were more than we'd bargained for. And the bastards didn't even have any reason to expect trouble from us.''

"Yes, they did," Katz corrected. "The terrorists had hit enough vehicles before to establish a pattern. If they have a commander worth a pinch of salt he would expect the Army to have someone 'riding shotgun' in the trucks. They just weren't prepared for the sort of deadly reception we gave them.''

"I don't see any point in trying to bait them again," Manning said. "They've been invulnerable until now. After losing five men, they'll probably assume it's too risky and try something else in the future.''

"Maybe yes," Encizo said, "maybe no.''

"Wouldn't you change tactics?" Arness asked.

"I'm not a terrorist," the Cuban explained. "They don't always do the logical thing. Hell, Colonel, we're dealing with fanatics. Terrorists can be bookworms raised on Karl Marx, ex-military commandos trying to overthrow a country or absolute lunatics who actually *want* to die for a cause and take as many other lives as possible with them in the process. There's no way to predict the actions of such people.''

"May I see those reports?" Katz asked. Arness passed the folder to the Israeli. "I'm inclined to agree with Manning in this case. The terrorists appear to be quite professional. I'd say they'll change their tactics. Better continue to have armed escorts with vehicles just to be safe.''

''That means we'd better change our tactics of trying to deal with them too,'' McCarter suggested.

''And what do you five hotshots plan to do now?'' O'Connor demanded.

''That's why we're having this meeting,'' Katz answered as he leafed through the documents. ''To decide a new plan of action.''

''I'm still wondering why the terrorists have always taken the trucks and jeeps and uniforms of their victims,'' Ohara said. ''there must be a reason.''

''Wait a minute,'' Katz declared, looking at a grainy photograph on a BND report. ''This face seems familiar.''

McCarter stepped closer and looked over the Israeli's shoulder at the poor reproduction of a lantern-jawed man with light hair. ''How can you be sure?''

''I'm not,'' Katz admitted. ''But I still think I've seen this man's picture before.''

''Is it one of the men the BND couldn't identify?'' Manning inquired.

''Yes,'' the Israeli said. ''Perhaps I could be sure if I saw a better photo of the man or perhaps the body itself. . . .''

A telephone mounted on the wall rang. Colonel Arness answered it.

''Hello, Colonel Bohler,'' the Army Intel man said after the caller identified himself. ''You have a lead?''

Every man in the room turned to Arness. The colonel's face was aglow with excitement.

"Yes." Arness spoke into the phone, but his eyes were on the men of Phoenix Force. "They're here, Colonel...." He listened for almost a full minute. "Yes, I'll tell them. Thank you, *mein herr*."

Arness hung up and addressed the others. "Colonel Bohler has just told me that GSG-Nine has located a very large cell of the German Red Army Faction in a Bavarian farmhouse twenty kilometers south of Munich. There's positively no room for error because GSG-Nine had an agent infiltrated among the ranks of the terrorists. He relayed this information to Bohler personally."

"My God!" O'Connor exclaimed. "We've got the bastards now."

"Bohler wants you five to meet him in one hour," Arness continued. "You're invited to join the raid on the farmhouse."

"When?" Ohara asked.

"Tonight," Arness replied.

"Wouldn't miss it for the world," McCarter assured him.

"So it's finally going to end." O'Connor sighed with relief.

"Maybe," Manning said. "We'll find out tonight."

6

Der Einenhorn was a typical West German bar—identical to an American tavern except the jukebox and television set tried to drown each other out in German instead of English and the customers played *fußball* machines rather than billiards.

Heinz Ritter had selected a small table in a corner facing the door. A nervous, chain-smoking man with a thinning hairline, he puffed cigarettes and drank three mugs of beer while he waited. Finally, a stocky man carried a glass of red wine to the table and joined Ritter.

"You're late, Herman," Ritter complained as he lit another cigarette.

"I'm cautious," Herman replied as he sat opposite Ritter. "I wanted to be certain you were not followed."

"Müller and the others trust me," Ritter declared. "My father was a member of ODESSA until the day he died. They all think I am a dedicated Nazi. None of them suspect I'm actually working for the SSD."

The Staats-Sicherheits-Dienst is the East German State Security Service. Like most other iron-curtain intelligence networks, the SSD is technically independent although it is supervised and manipulated by the Soviet KGB.

"True," the stocky SSD agent nodded. "But Müller knows you were educated in East Germany. That's where you earned your degree in physics and rocket systems. He must wonder about your loyalty, Heinz."

"He does not," Ritter insisted. "Müller thinks all sons of ODESSA will naturally embrace National Socialism as an infant seeks its mother's breast for nourishment. He believes we are all dedicated to his plan to unite Germany under a single government."

"That is not a bad idea," Herman mused. "Depending on who rules the government, *ja*? Have you discovered what these Nazi trash and the Baader-Meinhof fanatics plan to do?"

"Nein," Ritter said. "But they're planning something big, and it's to be directed against both the Americans and the Soviets in our country."

"Most of us would like to see the Russians driven out of East Germany," Herman said, "but whatever these lunatics have in mind is more apt to endanger our country than liberate it. If they succeed in attacking any Soviet bases, the Russians will simply respond by sending more troops into our homeland. We cannot allow these terrorists to succeed."

Ritter frowned. "Things may go sour before I can learn anything. Some of Müller's men tried to ambush another American Army truck. This time, the soldiers were ready for them: four Nazis and one former Baader-Meinhof gang member were killed.''

"The Americans surprise me at times," Herman said. "It's ironic that we, the Americans and even the damned BND now share a common goal against the same enemy. Too bad we cannot pool our forces and work together."

"The federal republic would hardly welcome us with open arms, comrade."

"True," Herman said. "What matters now is that Müller and the others still intend to carry out their mission, whatever it is."

"Ja," Ritter said. "The Nazis plan to launch some sort of special raid tonight, but it isn't the main operation. That's supposed to take place within the next four days."

"That doesn't give you much time to find out what these *Schweinehunden* are going to do. Yet it does mean this business will soon be over. I'm certain you will be glad of that, Heinz."

"I've been mingling with Nazis for more than a year," Ritter said. "Working undercover, infiltrating these murderous scum, has been the most nerve-racking experience I have ever had to endure. *Ja*, I will be very glad when this is over and I can return home."

"Your efforts will not go unrewarded, comrade," Herman assured him. "I am told you are to receive a promotion to captain and Herr

Wolf will personally award you the Order of the Red Flag.''

Ritter nodded, but he was not excited by Herman's lure of promotions and awards. One must survive to appreciate such things, and Ritter was more concerned with staying alive than with receiving recognition from the very people who had placed him in such a dangerous situation.

The only award I want, he thought, is my life.

7

Keio Ohara looked through the infrared Starlite viewer and slowly scanned the farmhouse and run-down old barn. The infrared turned the darkness of midnight into twilight and served as a powerful telescope, allowing the Japanese to examine the farm from a safe distance.

Rafael Encizo, standing beside Ohara with a Heckler & Koch MP-5 SD1 machine pistol in his fists, thought about the others who had assembled in the apple orchard a quarter of a mile from the farmhouse. Besides the other men of Phoenix Force, Colonel Bohler and forty highly trained GSG-Nine antiterrorists were present.

"I think we're ready," the Cuban commented.

"I certainly hope so," Ohara said quietly. "There are two sentries patrolling the area— armed with AK-47 assault rifles and what appear to be infrared scopes mounted to the barrels. Shall we tell the others?"

"I'm sure they'll be thrilled with the news," Encizo muttered.

Colonel Bohler was not pleased with their report, but he was not alarmed either. Dressed in camouflage black with matching beret and a Walther P-38 in a hip holster, Bohler looked as though he was ready to charge alone into the enemy stronghold.

"So they have automatic weapons," he said. "So do we. Yet why take chances with these scum? We've got grenade launchers and enough shells to blow that house to hell."

Gary Manning, also clad in black combat fatigues and armed to the teeth, turned to Bohler. The Canadian carried a big steel pistol in a shoulder holster under his left armpit. The Wildey 9mm Winchester Magnum was a monstrous handgun with a 15-round capacity. Manning also carried an assortment of grenades, and a black ditty bag full of explosives hung from his hip.

"We want to try to take some of the terrorists alive, Colonel," the Canadian said.

"And we will," Bohler replied. "But I have no intention of risking lives unless it is necessary. We can surround the farm, fire tear-gas grenades through the windows and order the terrorists to surrender. If they refuse, we'll blow them apart. The agent who infiltrated the group slipped away earlier today and there are no hostages inside the farmhouse—just two different breeds of terrorist filth."

"Two?" McCarter asked.

"*Ja,*" Bohler explained. "Some of the terrorists are Arabs, Syrians. Members of a splinter group calling themselves the Palestinian Protection Front."

"I wonder why they're doing their 'protecting' here in West Germany," Yakov Katzenelenbogen commented as he checked his Uzi submachine gun. He also carried a .45-caliber Colt Commander on his left hip and plenty of grenades and ammo on his belt.

"Colonel Bohler," Manning said as he opened an aluminum rifle case to remove an Anschutz .22-caliber air rifle, "we'd like to handle this our way."

"And how does your way differ from mine?" Bohler asked.

"Ours will not endanger the lives of your men, Colonel," Ohara answered, checking an H&K MP-5 SD2 submachine gun supplied by GSG-Nine. He had already slid a cocked and locked .45-caliber MatchMaster autoloader into a hip holster.

"Ludwig," Katz said, "if you alert the terrorists in advance, they'll have time to destroy documents, stolen merchandise, records, whatever. If these are the terrorists we came to Germany to find, we don't want to give them a second for cover-up."

"How do you want to handle it, Yakov?" Bohler asked.

"We'll go in and hit the terrorists fast," Encizo stated, as he pulled a Gerber Mark 1 combat dagger from its sheath and checked the edge of his thumb. The Cuban still carried the S&W .38 as a backup piece, but he had also borrowed a Heckler & Koch 9mm VP70Z pistol. A double-action mechanical marvel, the fine quality handgun had an 18-round capacity.

"Just the five of you?" Bohler asked with surprise. "You are aware there are twenty-seven terrorists in that building?"

"Hell," McCarter scoffed, screwing a foot-long silencer into the threaded barrel of his M-10. "That's not even six to one."

"Do we have your permission to do this our way, Ludwig?" Katz asked.

"Very well," the German agreed. "But make certain you all take gas masks. If any shooting occurs, we can lob in some tear-gas grenades to give you an edge."

"Good idea," Manning said.

"After we launch the gas," Bohler continued, "we'll wait one full minute before we move in. Don't expect us to let you have all the glory."

Katz smiled. "Your agent said there are some terrorists stationed inside the barn as well as the house, correct?"

"About half a dozen," Bohler confirmed. "But he isn't certain what they have for weapons. He didn't see the inside of the barn, perhaps some of the stolen U.S. Army vehicles are inside."

"We'll find out soon enough," McCarter remarked. "We've already talked over how we want to handle this, chaps. Any last-minute suggestions?"

"Let's all get drunk when this is over," Encizo replied, working the bolt of his MP-5 machine gun.

A FULL MOON SHONE on the farm as the men of Phoenix Force crept forward. They had decided in advance on their course of action and each man knew what he had to do. First, the sentries had to be dealt with.

Gary Manning, the Force's best rifleman, had been assigned to take out the first guard. He had brought the Anschutz along for just such an emergency. One of the finest air guns in the world, the Anschutz had a range of more than 100 yards. The Canadian had attached an infrared scope similar to the Starlite scanner in order to assure accuracy.

He approached the sentry, crawling on his belly until he was certain he was close enough to hit the terrorist. Manning assumed a prone position and looked into the scope. When the cross hairs met the target's left ear, the Canadian sharpshooter squeezed the trigger.

The Anschutz barely whispered a report, propelling a steel dart powered by a CO_2 cartridge. The dart struck the sentry in the side of the neck, immediately injecting a valium solution into the man's jugular. The sentry cried out weakly and tried to unsling his AK-47. The sedative rapidly churned through his bloodstream, reaching his brain in less than four seconds. The man crumpled to the ground, unconscious.

The other sentry heard the groan and turned toward the sound, pulling his assault rifle from his shoulder. He saw his comrade fall and immediately scanned the area for an enemy target. When he spotted Manning still sprawled on the grass with the single-shot air rifle, he raised his weapon.

A hand suddenly clamped over the man's mouth. The sentry tried to trigger his Kalashnikov to alert his comrades inside the house. Hot agony poured up his arm as if lava had entered his veins. Something bit into his hand. The guard glanced down in time to see the slashing blade of a knife and his severed index finger falling to the ground.

Then a piercing pain filled his right kidney and he convulsed wildly in the strong grip of his assailant. Finally, the knife struck a third time, slicing his throat open in a single swift stroke. Rafael Encizo released the dying sentry. The man's twitching body dropped.

Phoenix Force advanced quickly, Manning and McCarter heading toward the barn while the others moved toward the house. A light was on in the kitchen at the back of the house.

While Encizo crept to the front door, Yakov and Keio Ohara moved to the back. The curtains on the kitchen window were drawn, but a space between them allowed the tall Japanese to peek inside. He saw a beefy, long-haired terrorist seated at a card table, leafing through a porno magazine and sipping coffee laced with peppermint schnapps.

"Kamerad," Katz moaned at the door, speaking flawless German. "Comrade, I am sick. Open the door, *bitte*. I need help."

"Was ist das Scheisser?" the unsympathetic Red Army goon growled.

He stomped across the room and yanked the door open. The man barely had a chance to see Keio Ohara's arm rocket forward.

A *seiken* karate punch slammed into the point of the goon's chin. The blow knocked the terrorist backward five feet. Ohara followed his opponent and lashed a snap kick to his genitals. The German gasped and doubled up in agony. Ohara stepped closer and struck his victim behind the ear with the side of his hand. The terrorist fell to the floor in a heap.

Yakov Katzenelenbogen aimed the muzzle of his silencer-equipped Uzi at the doorway that led to a darkened room beyond, while Ohara knelt beside the unconscious terrorist, binding his wrists and ankles with plastic riot cuffs.

"Donnerwetter," a surly voice complained, from the next room.

A man dressed in a pair of dirty undershorts, with a tangled mess of uncombed hair on his head and a Russian-made Makarov pistol in his fist, appeared in the doorway.

"Was tuest Du, Rolf?" he growled.

Then his sleep-blurred eyes opened wide with alarm when he found himself face to face with

Katz and his Uzi. The man tried to raise his Makarov. The Israeli opened fire. A 3-round burst of 9mm projectiles kicked the hapless terrorist back. He tripped over another Red Army thug lying on the floor, then crashed on yet another comrade who cried out in surprise and anger, unaware that it was a corpse that had fallen on him. Numerous voices could be heard as the terrorists in the next room, two of them female, were abruptly roused from their slumber.

The thugs got off the floor, many clutching weapons. Katz did not hesitate. He fired a quick volley into the sleeping quarters next-door and ducked back from the doorway. Two voices, a man's and a woman's, screamed in agony while other terrorists responded by returning fire.

Bullets splintered the doorway and sizzled into the kitchen, chopping into walls and ricocheting off an old rust-spotted stove. A stray round struck a coffee maker, splitting it open, spilling hot dark-brown liquid on the floor.

Yakov glanced at Ohara. The Japanese cocked his head toward the back door and Katz nodded in agreement. He fired another long burst from his Uzi into the next room to give Ohara enough time to bolt outside.

RAFAEL ENCIZO raised a boot and slammed it into the front door.

The lock burst and the door swung open.

More terrorists had been sleeping in the front room, but the gunshots had roused them. Their attention was already directed toward the kitchen, and because everyone's ears were ringing, no one noticed the Cuban until it was too late.

Encizo's H&K MP-5 erupted in a deadly spray of 9mm rounds. Five bullets ripped a terrorist's back from left kidney to right shoulder blade, snapping his spine and hurtling him across the room. Another turned and received a trio of slugs in the throat and jaw. A third Red Army killer, a dumpy woman with a pimple-laced face, received four rounds in her chest.

Encizo retreated toward a staircase as some of the terrorists turned their attention—and their weapons—in his direction. A half-naked man suddenly charged down the stairs with a Soviet-made PPS machine gun in his hands. He spotted Encizo and tried to draw a bead on the huddled Cuban, when his own comrades opened fire. Bullets pulverized the Arab's bare legs. He screamed as he fell forward, absorbing more rapid-fire slugs as he tumbled down the stairs.

A window exploded in the dining room and another hailstorm of 9mm slugs leveled terrorists as Keio Ohara fired from outside the house. The terrorist machine gunners who had accidentally wasted the Palestinian Protection Front clod, suddenly met their own death.

Glass shattered in another window in the front room and a smoking projectile hit the floor. The tear-gas grenade immediately spewed a dense cloud throughout the house. Terrorists coughed and spit and stumbled into one another, trying to find their elusive targets as their eyes filled with tears and mucus bubbled from their nostrils.

DAVID MCCARTER and Gary Manning had reached the barn. After a quick recon they knew the large front doors and the hayloft on the second story were the only entrances or exits to the building. While the Englishman stood guard with his Ingram held ready, Manning opened his ditty bag and removed a quarter pound of Composition Four.

As Manning removed a pencil detonator from his pocket and prepared to insert it into the C-4, gunshots erupted from the farmhouse.

"The fucking balloon went up already," Manning muttered.

Alarmed voices inside the barn confirmed that time was quickly running out. McCarter glanced at Manning as the Canadian adjusted the timing mechanism of the detonator.

"Jesus," the Briton growled, "do you have to be so bloody slow."

"If I rush something like this I might blow us both to bits," Manning rasped. "At least then I wouldn't have to listen to you constantly belly-aching."

Without warning, the wooden shutters of the hayloft directly above their heads burst open and the snout of a weapon jutted forward. The muzzle pointed into the night and the rattling fury of rapid fire accompanied a streak of orange flame.

Great bloody damn, McCarter thought. The bastards have a machine gun nest up there.

The GSG-Nine gas grenades had already been lobbed into the house, and Colonel Bohler's men were beginning to advance. They would march right into the machine gun and be cut to pieces.

8

The battle in the farmhouse continued to rage. A Red Army Faction goon and one of the PPF killers rushed Yakov Katzenelenbogen's position in the kitchen. Armed with Skorpion machine pistols, the terrorists fired into the room as they crossed the threshold. The German threw himself in a low roll across the floor while the Syrian supplied cover fire. The pair blasted countless holes in the walls, punctured the side of a cheap refrigerator and tore a set of cabinets to pieces.

The only human flesh their bullets found, however, belonged to the bound and helpless German terrorist who lay on the floor.

The two guncocks then noticed the open outside door and the green blue object that had been tossed into the room. Before either men could react, the grenade exploded. The building trembled as both terrorists were torn limb from limb.

Rafael Encizo, wearing his M-17 gas mask, looked through the Plexiglas lenses up the stairwell. A dense gray fog at the head of the stairs told the Cuban that GSG-Nine gas grenades had also been lobbed into the next story.

Downstairs, only one terrorist remained on his feet and he presented little threat, having discarded his weapon to stagger about with both hands clamped over his eyes while he coughed uncontrollably.

Keio Ohara appeared beside the disabled terrorist, looking like a being from another planet—his face covered by a gas mask with snoutlike filters and bug-eyed lenses. Ohara's right hand swung like an ax, chopping the German's collarbone. The man's body buckled forward and Ohara's knee rose to connect with his opponent's face. The blow straightened the terrorist's back and set him up for the devastating sidekick. Ohara launched into the German's midsection. The man crashed into a wall, bounced and fell unconscious.

A figure bolted toward Encizo. The Cuban whirled, pointing his H&K MP-5 at the shape. Then he recognized the Uzi submachine gun held in the man's left hand, cradled by an artificial extremity with a three-pronged hook. Katz had also put on his gas mask, and he appeared even more alien with his prosthetic arm and the silencer-equipped Uzi.

"How are the numbers falling, Rafael?" the Israeli inquired, his voice muffled by the gas-mask filters.

"All the enemies on this floor are down for the count, but I think we've still got company upstairs."

As if to confirm the Cuban's theory, a voice cried out from upstairs in Arabic, a language Katz understood.

"Fedayeen," the Israeli shouted as loudly as his mask allowed. *"Ti-sah Idni."*

A hawk-faced Arab with a Russian PPS machine gun in his fists leaned over the upstairs railing. He stared through tear-clouded eyes, trying to locate his fellow PPF member. Katz and Encizo opened fire. A dozen 9mm-rounds ripped into the terrorist. The cascade of bullets spun the Arab around, his Soviet chatterbox flying from his grasp. The PPF hitman fell against the railing and slumped to the floor in a lifeless lump.

"You've got five seconds to surrender," Katz called up the stairwell in German. He repeated the warning in Arabic.

"Nein. Nein," a voice cried feebly.

Three figures, two men and a woman, appeared at the head of the stairs. All had their empty hands clamped firmly on their heads as they staggered down the stairs to surrender.

GARY MANNING QUICKLY ADJUSTED the detonator on the C-4 quarter-pounder to ten seconds. He jogged to the front doors of the barn. Meanwhile, David McCarter raised his Ingram and aimed at the hayloft.

The silenced M-10 machine pistol coughed violently and spat a 3-round burst into the opening around the barrel of the machine gun. Nine-millimeter bullets smashed into the terrorist operating the gun. Hollowpoint slugs shredded the man's face and blasted apart the back of his skull. When the enemy machine gun fell silent, McCarter quickly yanked a SAS-issue concussion grenade from his belt and pulled the pin.

Before the other terrorists could take over for the machine gunner, the Briton hurled the canister into the hayloft. McCarter threw himself to the ground and covered his head with his arms. The grenade exploded with a terrific roar. Dust, dried hay and spent cartridge casings spewed from the loft. A heavy object fell to earth less than a foot from where McCarter lay. He turned to see the battered body of an unconscious terrorist.

No sooner had Manning placed the C-4 pack in front of the barn than one of the doors began to swing open. The Canadian raced away from the entrance and dived, executing a fast shoulder roll.

"Schweinehund," a Red Army Faction killer snarled as he emerged from the barn in time to see Manning rolling.

He fired a hasty round that hissed inches above Manning's tumbling body. Another terrorist positioned himself behind a Heckler & Koch HK21A1 machine gun mounted on a 1102 tripod at the door. The first German hood tried to aim his Makarov pistol at Manning for another shot, but the Phoenix Force member had already scrambled around the corner out of view.

Ten seconds were up.

The C-4 bomb exploded at the feet of the two Red Army fanatics. The open barn door was blown off its hinges by the blast and the other door swung drunkenly on broken mounts. Dismembered chunks of terrorists and mangled bits of metal were scattered across the ground. A full minute passed, then a lone terrorist staggered outside and collapsed in the dust.

HALF AN HOUR LATER, a fleet of military ambulances had hauled away the dead and wounded terrorists. GSG-Nine commandos escorted the ambulances to the Army hospitals where the survivors would receive treatment. Colonel Bohler joined Phoenix Force in the debris-littered front room of the farmhouse.

Naturally, the place was a shambles: blankets and mattresses were strewed across the floor where the terrorists had slept before the raid interrupted their slumber; furniture had been chipped and shredded by bullets; plaster was ripped from the walls and blood-stains were everywhere.

When the single lamp to survive the carnage was turned on, the men discovered a large map of the Federal Republic of Germany tacked on the wall. There were also two more detailed street maps of Munich and Bonn. Several red X marks had been drawn on the city diagrams.

"I found some files, if you can call them that, upstairs," Yakov told Bohler as he handed the colonel a bundle of notebooks and scratch paper. "We now know why the German Red Army Faction and the Palestinian Protection Front joined forces."

"Well, don't keep us in suspense," McCarter said, sitting in a bullet-ripped armchair.

"The notes explain the target areas on the maps. They are German military installations, synagogues, restaurants and jewelry stores as well as the Israeli embassy in Bonn. The terrorists intended to strike a blow against the governments of West Germany and Israel."

"By blowing up jewelry stores and restaurants?" Rafael Encizo asked.

"The businesses are owned by Jews," Katz explained. "To the PPF that would be attacking Israel...at least, it would be a good enough excuse in their opinion."

"Then we did not hit the right group of terrorists," Bohler said, frowning, looking at the maps with dismay.

"If I may correct you, Colonel," Keio Ohara said, "we did not find the terrorists we came to your country in search of. Yet the group we have put out of business tonight also planned great evil. There is no need to regret their destruction."

"Destruction indeed." Bohler looked about the room. "I thought you wanted to take some of the terrorists alive."

"Some of them are," McCarter remarked. "Well, sort of."

"Perhaps after we question the survivors—when they're able to talk—they will lead us to the men we're after," Bohler said.

"I doubt that, Colonel," Manning said. "We didn't find any evidence to link this outfit with the people who have been attacking the American servicemen. There are no U.S. Army vehicles in the barn, no American uniforms or ID cards, and every terrorist was armed with Soviet and Czech weapons except for a few Heckler & Koch military arms that were probably stolen from national military bases."

"Guess you can consider our efforts tonight as an extra," Encizo told Bohler. "We helped you take care of a little local trouble before it could spread."

"Ja," the German colonel said. "But we're no closer to solving our mutual problem than we were before."

"Well," McCarter shrugged, "you can't have everything."

9

Rudolf Kortze screwed a nine-inch silencer into his Walther PPK as he sat behind the steering wheel of a stolen BMW. The blond terrorist glanced over his shoulder at the two men in the back seat. Once again, he was working with Gunther, the gaunt sadist, and another Nazi named Ricardo Dieter.

"The others should be here soon," Kortze remarked. "You both know what to do?"

"How will we get inside the buildings?" Dieter asked.

The bastard son of a former SS officer and a Brazilian girl, Dieter did not look like a typical Nazi. His skin was brown, his eyes dark and his hair jet black. However, he had been raised with the dogma of National Socialism and he was just as fanatical as any member of ODESSA.

"Our Baader-Meinhof allies managed to have keys made from clay imprints of the locks," Kortze replied. "The keys have already been tested during a recon mission last week. We will have no problem getting inside. Just remember not to draw your weapons until we are in the building. The American military police frequently patrol this area.''

"So?" Gunther said, smiling. "We can kill them too."

"Nein," Kortze said firmly. "We don't want to attract attention, Gunther."

Gunther nodded.

The three Nazis were parked at an area reserved for American officers above the rank of captain. They were concerned only with a cottagelike house and a single apartment building separated from the other buildings at the military housing center.

"That's them," Kortze declared, when two more cars drove into the visitors' parking lot.

Kortze put his Walther in a black briefcase and emerged from the car, followed by Gunther and Dieter. Four ODESSA agents and two former Baader-Meinhof gang members stepped out of the other two vehicles. The six men carried cases, and all wore dark blue or black business suits and neckties. To a casual observer, they appeared to be a collection of young executives or salesmen. Few would suspect that the neatly dressed, clean-cut men might be terrorists.

They did not speak. Each knew his role in the operation. Kortze was the group commander and he would see to the most important target site. Otto Schroder was second-in-command, and he would handle the second target.

Kortze led Gunther and Dieter to the first cottage while Schroder escorted the rest of the men to the apartment building. Although Kortze's single target was the most important, Schroder's required more manpower. Kortze removed a key from his pocket and inserted it into the door of the cottage. The lock clicked open.

Kortze, Dieter and Gunther entered the unlit interior and closed the door. All three men wore thin plastic film glued to the tips of their fingers to avoid leaving prints.

Dieter pulled a small penlight from his pocket and a Mauser HSC pistol, with a silencer attached, from a specially designed shoulder holster rig. The Nazi had handled such covert operations before. His appearance made him valuable in South America where he had once assassinated two Mossad agents who were trying to locate the elusive lair of the infamous Dr. Joseph Mengele.

The penlight beam soon found a stairway. The trio headed for it, Kortze taking the lead. They carefully mounted the steps, favoring the edges close to the banister, which are less apt to creak underfoot.

At the head of the stairs, they found three rooms. One was a small bathroom, the door standing open. Kortze selected the door on the left of the bathroom. He turned the knob slowly and looked into the room.

Two figures lay in a double bed. The head of a middle-aged man, whose dark hair was streaked with silver, rested on a pillow beside the bleached-blond head of his wife. Kortze was relieved that he had found the adults' bedroom. The American colonel had two young sons. Kortze disliked killing children—even American children.

Neither the sleeping man nor his wife stirred as the terrorist drew closer. He aimed his Walther PPK at the woman's head and pressed the silencer muzzle into her yellow hair before he squeezed the trigger.

The *phut* of the suppressed shot and the woman's convulsions of death awoke her husband with a start. He opened his mouth and suddenly felt a cylinder of hard metal thrust between his lips. Kortze pumped a .380 round through the roof of the American's mouth and shot him again between the eyes.

Another sound suppressor rasped from the other bedroom. Gunther had decided to take care of the American children by himself. A small boy's voice cried out, only to be silenced by a muffled bullet. Gunther giggled with delight.

One day, Kortze thought grimly, I shall have the pleasure of killing you, Gunther.

But for now, ODESSA needed the sadistic gunman.

10

"Colonel O'Connor is dead," Matthew Arness announced.

The intelligence officer addressed Colonel Ludwig Bohler and three members of Phoenix Force—Gary Manning, Rafael Encizo and David McCarter.

They were all startled to learn of O'Connor's death. While the NATO Security officer had not endeared himself to the men of Phoenix Force, he had been on their side and, in his own way, the colonel had been trying to do what he thought best for the defense of his country.

"How did it happen?" Manning asked, crossing the room to the coffee maker.

"Murder," Arness replied. "Someone entered O'Connor's home and shot him to death. They also killed his wife and kids. O'Connor's family wasn't the only one they hit. Two other field-grade officers in the housing complex—a lieutenant colonel and a major—and their families—were also murdered."

Arness pulled off his service cap, looking as if he might rip it apart out of sheer frustration and anger. "It was a goddamn bloodbath. Eleven killed, mostly women and children."

"It must have happened while we were cleaning out that nest of Red Army Faction terrorists," Bohler remarked. "The band of terrorists responsible for the attacks on American military personnel didn't wait for us to get back to them. You were right, Gary. They changed their tactics, but none of us could have guessed they'd do something like this."

"Did they hit O'Connor because he was an American serviceman or because he was with NATO Security?" McCarter wondered aloud.

"Or because he was associated with us," Manning added. "Any idea how the terrorists got into O'Connor's home?"

"No sign of forced entry," Colonel Arness replied. "The front door of the apartment building where the other families were killed wasn't forced either, although one of the doors to an apartment was pried open, probably with a crowbar."

"And no one saw anything suspicious?" Encizo asked. "No one heard anything unusual?"

"Nothing. There were no reports of gunshots or screams and no other evidence of violence. If a maid hadn't found O'Connor this morning, we probably wouldn't even know he'd been killed."

"The terrorists must have used silencers," Encizo commented.

"What the hell are the bastards up to?" Manning said. "There must be a reason for their actions. They're too professional to be acting randomly. They're preparing for something."

"The uniforms and ID—they were taken from the previous victims. What about this time?" Encizo asked.

"The Criminal Investigation Department personnel in charge of the investigation of the murders already checked on that," Arness said. "They told me none of the victims' wallets were stolen. The intruders also left O'Connor's NATO Security badge and they left whole closets full of uniforms untouched."

"If there were closets full of uniforms," McCarter said, "then no one can be certain one or two aren't missing. I'm sure they all had extra rank insignia as well."

"Do you honestly believe the killers are going to all this trouble to steal some uniforms?" Bohler asked. "O'Connor was right when he said one can buy such clothing from pawnshops here in Germany."

"And if they intended to have someone impersonate Colonel O'Connor in order to sneak into the NATO 222 site," Arness added, "wouldn't they take his security badge and military ID? And anyway, the sentries know who goes in and out of the site on a regular basis. They'd spot a phony O'Connor."

"Besides," McCarter muttered, "the NATO guards have probably been told about his murder by now."

"All of this connects somehow," Manning insisted, staring into his coffee cup like a fortune-teller trying to read tea leaves. "Wait a minute," he said suddenly. "What about those two MPs? The pair that were murdered last month. Weren't they attached to NATO Security?"

"That's right," Arness replied. "Although I don't know which site or what their clearance was."

"Find out," Manning told him. "I have a suspicion you'll discover they were attached to NATO 222, same as O'Connor."

"What is NATO 222?" Encizo asked. "A missile site?"

"Well," Arness said, "that's not exactly a state secret anymore. Yes, NATO 222 contains about forty missile silos for our new Warhawks."

"By the way," Bohler interrupted, "where is my old friend Yakov and the tall Japanese fellow?"

"They're probably in Austria by now," Encizo answered.

"Austria?" Arness asked in surprise. "What are they doing there?"

"You remember how Yakov thought he recognized one of the terrorists who attacked Rafael and David the other day?" Manning asked. "Well, he went down to the morgue to get a look at the dead man so he could see what the guy really looked like."

"He then called us and said he had a hunch," McCarter said, "but he'd have to talk to a chap in Vienna to see if there was anything to it. Since we couldn't all run off to check a lead when most of the action seems to be here in Germany, Keio volunteered to meet Yakov at the Frankfurt airport. He's probably running all over Vienna like a typical Japanese tourist, carrying four cameras and taking pictures of everything he sees with each one."

"Austria." Arness sighed. "I hope your friend knows what he's doing."

"Don't worry," Encizo assured him. "Keio is very good with a camera."

NICHOLAS MAVROS DID NOT LIKE the arrangement. Like hundreds of other Greeks, he had been lured to West Germany by the country's high standard of living and stable economy. A master printer by trade, he had little trouble finding employment, but the available jobs failed to pay a salary that supported his expensive cocaine habit.

Mavros fell into a new career as a professional forger. Producing phony passports, drivers' licenses, national identification cards and work permits was child's play for a man of his abilities. His customers included underworld gangsters from four countries, embezzlers, police informers and, most of all, terrorists.

He had known Norbert and Helga Konner for more than ten years and had done a great deal of business with the Baader-Meinhof gang in the 1970s. Mavros trusted Norbert and Helga as far as he could ever trust people in their profession. However, he did not like the men who had accompanied the couple that day. Although the tall silver-haired stranger and his blond associate wore business suits, they had a military manner that disturbed Mavros. He was accustomed to dealing with pseudointellectuals like the Konners, not soldiers disguised in civilian clothing.

"These are excellent, Herr Mavros," Heinrich Müller announced, after examining several blue and orange badges.

"It was not difficult, *mein herr*," the Greek replied nervously. "With the orange badges to use for a model and the photos of the blue badges, it was easy to forge both types."

"You are certain they will pass as genuine?" Müller asked, casting a quick glance at Rudolf Kortze.

"Ja, mein herr," Mavros assured him. "Actually, the standard identification cards for the United States Army personnel were more difficult to reproduce. However, only an expert would be able to spot them as forgeries."

"Excellent, Herr Mavros." The Nazi nodded. "Tell me, how long have you been running this little covert printing business?"

Müller glanced around the room as if considering purchasing goods in a store. The basement was filled with large and small printing presses, photo- and color-copiers, plastic card punch machines and shelves of paper segregated by color and texture.

"Fifteen years," Mavros replied.

"But officially you are retired, *ja*?" the ODESSA commander asked, cocking a silver eyebrow.

Helga Konner tugged at her husband's sleeve. Norbert turned and looked into her distress-filled eyes. He solemnly shook his head and gently removed her hand from his arm.

"That is why I work here in my house," the Greek said. "Didn't Norbert and Helga explain that?"

"Indeed," Müller admitted. "So no one will miss you for some time. Correct?"

"What...what do you mean...?" Mavros rasped.

"You know what I mean," the Nazi said. "Like a steer in a slaughterhouse, you smell blood."

"No..." Mavros whispered hoarsely as he backed away from Müller, his lips trembling in fear.

Kortze, who had stealthily moved behind the forger, removed a garrote from his pocket. He deftly swung the steel wire over Mavros's head. The young Nazi yanked the wooden handles of the strangling cord and tightened the loop firmly around the forger's neck.

"I'm sorry, Herr Mavros," Müller said sadly. "You really did excellent work."

Kortze pulled the garrote and gave it a hard twist to the right. The Greek's throat was sliced open and his spinal cord snapped. The corpse of Nicholas Mavros relieved itself. Urine poured down his pant leg, forming a puddle at his shoes. Kortze unwound the garrote from his victim's neck and the lifeless shell that had been Nicholas Mavros slumped to the floor.

"*Why*, Norbert?" Helga demanded, seizing her husband's arm. She pulled him about to face her. "Why?"

"You know why, damn it," Konner said sharply. "Our mission is too important to allow anything to jeopardize it. I told you what would have to be done to Nicholas. I asked you not to come, but you insisted. It is done, Helga. Nothing can change that."

"Your behavior surprises me, Frau Konner," Müller remarked. "When you were with the Baader-Meinhof gang you and your husband kidnapped German businessmen, assassinated people—most of them Germans—and you sabotaged military and civilian buildings with explosives that killed more Germans. But that was all acceptable because it was part of your war against capitalism, right? Why then does the death of one man, a forger, disturb you?"

"Nicholas was a friend," Norbert Konner said. "Certainly, you can understand the difference."

"Of course," Müller agreed. "It is easier to kill strangers."

"You don't need us anymore, do you?" Konner asked.

"Take your wife to the car and wait for us," the Nazi said. "Rudolf and I will take care of everything here."

Müller watched Konner escort Helga up the narrow stairway from the basement. Kortze approached his commander.

"She is a weak link in our operation," he said. "Both of them are weak."

"Frau Konner no longer believes in causes," Müller said. "All she has left is her love for her husband. That is why she can be trusted. Konner is a dreamer. He is intelligent enough to realize his former philosophy was false, but he is still a dreamer who has stubbornly tried to alter his old beliefs to fit a new cause."

"But we are not dreamers," Kortze remarked. "ODESSA is for doers, not dreamers."

"Dreamers can assist us with their ideas and visions," Müller said. "But we are the kind of men who make dreams a reality."

He glanced down at the corpse of Nicholas Mavros and added, "Even if it requires a few nightmares."

11

David McCarter's prediction that Keio Ohara would behave like a typical tourist in Vienna proved to be only a slight exaggeration. The Japanese had brought a camera and made liberal use of it as he and Yakov Katzenelenbogen rode in the back of a taxicab from the airport.

Colonel Katzenelenbogen smiled as he watched Keio rapidly remove a spent roll of film from his camera and load a fresh one with the same quick precision he used when changing magazines for a weapon in combat. The normally inscrutable Japanese behaved like a small boy on his first visit to a zoo. Ohara was the youngest member of Phoenix Force and Katz was his eldest teammate, yet there was no generation gap between the two men.

The Israeli was not annoyed by his friend's youthful enthusiasm. Katz recalled the excitement he had felt when he first visited Vienna shortly after World War II. Ohara's attitude served to rekindle that original thrill.

Katz had given the driver directions to an apartment building, and now as they pulled up to the curb, he removed his wallet to pay the fare.

The driver did not suspect Katz was an amputee. Yakov wore a pair of pearl-gray gloves; the one on his right ''hand'' concealed a special five-fingered prosthetic device. Katz had chosen the contraption because it did not draw attention to his missing limb and it served a practical, potentially lethal, function as well.

Because he and Ohara had traveled to Austria via a civilian airline, Katz had been unable to bring any conventional firearms. Yet he was not unarmed. A .22 Magnum one-shot pistol was built into the steel prosthetic hand. The index finger was actually the barrel of the weapon, which Katz could fire by manipulating muscles in the stump of his right arm.

Keio Ohara had only one weapon at his disposal—his body. The Japanese was a fourth *dan* black belt karate expert and he also held a second *dan* black belt in judo. Calluses covered his knuckles, the result of years of training with a *makiwara* striking post. Ohara's fingertips and the sides of his hands were also tempered into deadly weapons. At close quarters, he did not need a gun to deal with an opponent.

The pair left the cab and walked to the apartment building. A fat woman in a baggy dress barely looked up from a magazine as she sat behind the front desk. Katz told her they wished to see Herr Wienberg. She gave him the man's apartment number and pointed to an elevator that resembled a bird cage.

They rode up the ancient shaft to the second floor and stepped into a narrow hallway. Katz located a door with the numeral 14 tacked on it and knocked.

The door opened and a wrinkled face looked up at them. Framed by a mane of uncombed white hair and an untrimmed beard, the wide-eyed, tight-lipped face could have belonged to a mad hermit. The shaggy head was attached to a frail body clothed in an old housecoat. The man sat in a wheelchair. A blanket across his lap failed to conceal that both his legs had been amputated below the knee.

"Yakov," Solomon Wienberg exclaimed. "*Gut Gott.* You have contacted me again, at last."

Katz had told Keio about Solomon Wienberg during their flight from Frankfurt to Vienna. Wienberg, a German Jew, had lost his family in Dachau, victims of Hitler's "Final Solution."

When the war ended, Wienberg longed to see the butchers of his family pay with their lives for their crimes. Although many Nazi leaders did not survive the war and others were executed after the Nuremburg Trials, a large number of supporters of Hitler's regime remained unaccounted for. Almost a thousand members of the Gestapo and the SS disappeared after Berlin fell. Some, like Adolf Eichmann, who was hanged in Ramla, Israel, in 1962, have been punished for their crimes. Others, such as Martin Bormann and Joseph Mengele, are still on the wanted list at Tel Aviv.

Wienberg had devoted his life to tracking down Nazi war criminals. He collected an enormous file on the Third Reich and received considerable information from organizations and individuals eager to see Nazi fugitives brought to justice. Wienberg frequently shared the most promising pieces of this data with Interpol and the Israeli embassy.

Yakov Katzenelenbogen had been a major in the Israeli army and a covert case officer for Mossad in the late 1950s. For a while, he was stationed at the embassy in Vienna. Katz and other Israeli agents investigated Wienberg's claims. Most proved to be false. However, occasionally Wienberg's leads paid off. Mossad caught five minor-league ex-SS members thanks to the Nazi hunter.

Then a series of events ruined Wienberg's credibility. In 1965, a group of Czechoslovakian *svazarm* amateur divers discovered some tar-coated boxes in Black Lake. The Czech government announced that the caches contained Nazi documents. Since such caches had previously been found in Lake Toplitz in Czechoslovakia in 1959—containing millions of counterfeit British bank notes the Nazis had planned to use in a plot to deflate England's economy—the discovery attracted a great deal of attention. The Czech Ministry for Foreign Affairs turned over several of the Black Lake documents to the American, British and French embassies in Prague. The documents were verified as authentic.

Wienberg was contacted by a former concentration-camp prisoner who belonged to the Svaz Protifasistickych Bojovniku—the Czechoslovakian Union of Fighters Against Facism. The Czech claimed that the Black Lake documents included information proving certain British and French statesmen and businessmen had collaborated with the Nazis during the war. Wienberg was outraged and used his popularity as a Nazi hunter to demand the prosecution of these "traitors to humanity." He also condemned the governments of Britain and France for covering up "treason which they must surely be aware of."

The "Nazi caches" from Black Lake proved to be a hoax. The Czech Intelligence Service and its KGB overseers had planted the boxes themselves. The documents examined by the embassies were indeed genuine, but they had been supplied by the Kremlin. The Communists had used the scheme for a clever "black propaganda" campaign. The Czech antifascists had also been used by the Department of Disinformation in order to create hostility against governments of the West.

Too late, Wienberg realized he had been duped. He was fortunate not to face charges of slander and libel for his accusations. However, the incident ruined the man as a Nazi hunter. He still tried to obtain information about war criminals, but Israel did not want to be associated with him after he caused such an international embarrassment.

Solomon Wienberg became a bitter shell of a man. In 1979 his body was ravaged by bone cancer. Both legs had to be amputated. He still lived in his apartment in Vienna, waiting for cancer to finally claim his life. Wienberg had little except a horrid past and a hopeless future.

Yakov Katzenelenbogen knew Wienberg had been consumed by hate and desire for revenge for almost forty years. These emotions had destroyed his life just as effectively as the cancer that infested his body. However, Wienberg was still one of the world's foremost authorities on the Third Reich and Nazi war criminals. If anyone could confirm or reject the Israeli's suspicions, it was Solomon Wienberg.

"I'm very pleased to see you again, Yakov," Wienberg said, as he wheeled himself to a coffee table. "Who is your friend? Is he Japanese?"

"He is trustworthy," Katz assured him.

"Japan and the Nazis were once allies...."

"Solomon," the Israeli said with a sigh. "Don't worry about my friend. I have a photograph of a man. Perhaps you can identify him for me."

Katz handed Wienberg the photo of the terrorist who had sparked his memory in Germany. The Nazi hunter examined the picture and gasped.

"This looks like Kapitan Ernst Scherhorn," Wienberg declared, shaking his head in disbelief.

"Scherhorn?" Katz frowned. "Wasn't he an officer in a *totenkopfverbande*?"

"Ja," Wienberg said. "He was in a Death's Head Unit in Sobibor, Poland. He was one of General Globonik's top executioners in that accursed concentration camp."

"Scherhorn vanished after the war, correct?" Katz asked.

"He's supposed to have traveled with Eichmann for a while," Wienberg answered. "Probably fled to South America. . . but this can't be Scherhorn's photograph. It is a recent picture, *ja*? Yet it appears to be Scherhorn as he looked forty years ago."

"Sins of the father," Katz remarked. "I believe this man was Scherhorn's son. He was killed in a gun battle with a couple of friends of mine."

"Then it has happened," Wienberg said with a quavering voice. "What we have feared most has happened. The nightmare has started once again. The Nazis have risen from the ashes."

"Nein, Solomon," Katz assured him. "It isn't the same. The Nazis are not a political power. None of them have been elected to public office. The National Socialist Party is outlawed in Germany. The Nazis have been

reduced to the level of common gangsters. My friends and I will stop them before they can succeed at whatever evil they are planning.''

ADOLF ZEIGLER LOOKED through a pair of Bushnell 8x21 binoculars. His teeth clashed in anger when he saw the two Phoenix Force warriors emerge from the apartment building. Although sixty-three years old, Zeigler was a strong man with enormous shoulders and incredibly powerful hands. He nearly broke the field glasses in two as a tremor of fury rode through his body.

"Colonel Katzenelenbogen of the filthy Jewish Mossad,'' he said.

"Are you certain, *Herr Obergruppenführer*?'' Hans Aufricht inquired. "I thought that Israeli *Schweinehund* has only one arm.''

"Have you never heard of prostheses?'' Zeigler replied. "No, perhaps you haven't. Believe me, I am certain that man is Katzenelenbogen. He was the team leader of the Mosad unit that hit the ODESSA headquarters in Southern France. Only a handful of our people escaped.''

Zeigler ran a hand over the long white scar that extended from his eyebrow to his cheek. His left eye was milky white and sightless. He indeed had reason to recall the Israeli colonel who had ripped open his face with a steel hook, blinding him in one eye.

Katz had also stabbed Zeigler in the chest

with a bayonet and left him for dead. But Adolf Zeigler did not die easily. He had survived the war and continued to fight for the Third Reich as an officer in ODESSA.

Zeigler had risen through the ranks to become the head of ODESSA's intelligence operations, the third highest position in the organization. One day, he vowed, he would inherit command of the Nazi party just as the Reich would reclaim control of a united Germany.

First, ODESSA had to succeed with its current operation., *Standartenführer* Müller, one of their best officers, had been placed in charge of the mission, but Zeigler had flown to Europe to personally check for anything that might have been overlooked that could jeopardize the operation.

He himself had ordered the surveillance of Solomon Wienberg's apartment, but he had not suspected anyone like Katzenelenbogen would be associated with the has-been Nazi hunter. Something would have to be done about the Israeli.

"I want Katzenelenbogen and his Oriental friend followed," Zeigler declared.

"But the Israeli could not possibly know about our operation. . ." Aufricht began.

"You must learn two things, Hans," the Nazi general told him. "*Nothing* is impossible, and *never* underestimate an enemy. We must find out if the Jewish pig is part of an effort to stop our mission in West Germany."

"And if there appears to be such a connection, do you want those two terminated?"

"Hans," Zeigler said, "do you really need to ask a question to which the answer is so obvious?"

12

Yakov Katzenelenbogen and Keio Ohara spent less than four hours in Vienna. They caught a flight back to the Federal Republic of Germany and arrived at the Frankfurt International Airport shortly after noon.

"All we learned was that the Nazis might be involved in the terrorism, but we still don't have any idea where to find them or what they're planning," Katz said to Keio, summing up their trip, as they walked through the terminal.

"We have encountered such problems in the past and we have always managed to solve them and accomplish our mission," Keio replied with confidence.

"But we weren't dealing with ODESSA," the Israeli stated. "I've had experience trying to hunt them down. ODESSA has forty years of practice at hiding from their enemies."

"A cobra is difficult to locate among the bamboo," Ohara replied, "yet it must raise its head and spread its hood before it strikes."

"For a young man, you are very wise, Keio," the Israeli said, smiling. "Let's share this pearl of philosophical wisdom with the others and see what we can come up with.''

The pair emerged from the airport and found a taxicab parked at the curb. Rudolf Kortze watched them through the windshield of a gray sedan in a parking lot across the street. Kortze started the engine of his car and picked up a radio transceiver.

"Team Two," he spoke into the mouthpiece. "This is Team One. Over."

"Team Two," Otto Schroder replied from the walkie-talkie. "We read you. Over."

"They have arrived," Kortze declared. "They're in a taxi marked Number Fourteen."

"Number Fourteen," Schroder repeated. "We are heading toward your location, driving West on *Pickestrasse*. Should we intercept the cab? Over."

"Nein," Kortze replied. "Stay on your present route and prepare to back us up if we need assistance. Over and out."

Kortze put the radio away and checked the silencer attached to his Walther PPK. Gunther leaned toward him from the back seat.

"It is fortunate that General Zeigler found out about this Israeli and his slant-eyed companion," Gunther said. "And we are lucky to be given the task of getting rid of them."

"Ja," Kortze snorted.

Kortze really wished Zeigler had taken care of the Mossad agent and the Japanese while they were still in Austria. Could it be the great Herr

Zeigler did not want to attract attention to ODESSA in Vienna because he would be in personal danger? Instead, the task and the danger had been passed on to Kortze and his men.

"All right," he told Gunther. "You know the plan. We want to attract as little attention to ourselves as possible. That won't be easy since we have to hit them in broad daylight in downtown Frankfurt."

"No problem," Gunther said, smiling as he raised his silencer-equipped Luger. "The driver of the cab is going to lose control of his vehicle and have a nasty accident."

KATZ AND OHARA RODE in the cab into the center of the city. Buses, streetcars and mopeds competed with the automobiles for space. Traffic in every major city in the Federal Republic of Germany tends to be hectic; Germans are notorious for speeding.

Frankfurt is an ideal example of the two faces of West Germany. Numerous old buildings and Gothic churches stand proudly on the same city block with skyscrapers and fast-food restaurants.

Anyone who believes the stereotype of Germans as cold and militaristic needs to take a trip to Frankfurt. Stores and taverns are usually operated by cheerful managers who are polite to customers in two or more languages. German police and military generally wear their hair longer than their American counterparts and they tend to ignore minor violations.

The stereotype of a prudish German society is an even bigger myth. Pornography is sold openly in bookstores, and there is virtually no censorship of German movies and television. Prostitution is legal. The women who practice prostitution receive regular medical inspections and pay taxes. Venereal disease has not escalated in West Germany as it has in the United States. Sexual assault is extremely rare, perhaps because there is a provision in the FRG law allowing for castration of violent sex offenders.

Yakov Katzenelenbogen thought about how much Germany had changed, as he and Ohara rode through the streets of Frankfurt. Pornography and antinuke protests by the Green Party are legal, but the Nazi party and its literature are banned. Germany is probably the most difficult country in the world for Nazis to operate in.

This fact nagged at the Israeli. Why would ODESSA be involved with some has-been terrorists from the Baader-Meinhof gang?

Glancing out the rear window, Katz suddenly saw a gray sedan closing in fast. He had noticed the same car following the cab after they left the airport. He turned to Keio.

"I know," the young warrior said, "we are being tailed."

"Looks like we've found that striking

cobra,'' the Israeli remarked. "A little sooner than we expected.''

"Perhaps we should tell the driver to let us out,'' Ohara suggested.

"Right,'' Katz agreed. "We don't want to endanger the man's life or the lives of other innocent bystanders.''

He was about to tell the driver to pull over when the gray sedan suddenly changed lanes and sped forward. The car drove alongside the cab. Katz glanced at the grim-faced blond driver behind the wheel of the sedan. A grinning goon stared from an open rear window, aiming a gun at the taxi.

"Achtung! Halt!" Katz shouted as he and Ohara ducked.

The warning was meant for the cabdriver, but it was given too late. Gunther had already trained his Luger on the cabbie and squeezed the trigger. The silenced pistol coughed. The driver's head recoiled as a 7.65mm bullet drilled through the base of his skull.

The cabbie slumped against the door, hands frozen on the wheel. The taxi swerved to the left and entered the lane for oncoming traffic. Horns sounded as cars headed straight for the cab.

Keio lunged over the backrest and seized the wheel, turning it to the right. The taxi swung out of the path of the charging traffic, narrowly missing a head-on collision with a VW minibus.

The sedan kept pace with the cab. Gunther

aimed his Luger at the Japanese. Katz suddenly appeared in the window. A gloved hand jutted forward, the index finger pointed at the Nazi gunman's gaunt face.

"Senile old Jew," Gunther said, laughing as he altered the aim of his P.08 to deal with the Israeli.

The tip of Katz's finger exploded in a yellow burst. Gunther felt a hard object strike the bridge of his nose. He heard the crack of the .22 Magnum and realized a bullet had sliced into his face.

Ohara spun the wheel sharply and swung the cab into the side of the sedan before Rudolf Kortze could speed away. Metal clashed and the Nazi fought to keep his car on the road. Ohara took advantage of Kortze's problem and swung his legs over the backrest onto the front seat of the taxi.

The Japanese shoved the dead cabbie aside and positioned himself behind the wheel. Kortze shot forward, the tires of his sedan burning rubber. A smile flickered across Keio's face as he stomped on the gas to give chase.

"Oh, God," Katz said, familiar with his partner's driving habits.

Keio Ohara was superbly disciplined and controlled—until he got behind the wheel of a car. Then a reckless and ruthless side of his personality surfaced. But at that moment, a madman at the wheel was exactly what they needed.

The cab roared after the Nazi's car, rapidly

gaining. Kortze sped around a corner too fast and lost control of his vehicle. The sedan smashed into the rear of a parked car. Metal scraped and glass from a headlight exploded. The sedan skidded into the path of a garbage truck.

Horns blared and voices screamed. Kortze turned the wheel desperately. He nearly avoided the truck, but the front fender of the larger vehicle tagged the sedan's frame. Kortze overreacted and steered the car over the curb of a sidewalk and into a bratwurst stand.

Clapboard burst apart and food was splattered in all directions. The operator of the stand tumbled across the sidewalk. As Ohara drove forward, he saw that the bratwurst man had rolled out of the way and no other innocents were nearby. He rammed the cab into the rear of the sedan. The Nazi's car slid along the sidewalk and slammed lengthwise into a streetlight.

Ohara immediately drove the taxi into the side of the disabled vehicle. A metallic crunch sounded and steel crumpled on impact. Glass smashed from the sedan's windows and steam sprayed from the cab's ruptured radiator.

Katz found himself on the floor in the back of the cab. He felt as if he had taken a ride inside an electric blender.

Ohara quickly opened the driver's door and raced outside. The Japanese leaped onto the hood of the cab and dashed along it to the sedan. He dived to the top of the enemy vehicle and rolled across the roof to the opposite side of the car. Keio almost landed on Rudolf Kortze as the Nazi staggered out the door, Walther PPK in his fist.

Kortze only glimpsed a shape that jumped from the car roof. He swung his pistol toward the Japanese, but he was not fast enough. Ohara's powerful hands snared his wrist and raised his arm skyward. Kortze pulled the trigger and his silenced PPK hissed at the clouds.

Ohara twisted the Nazi's arm and held it by the wrist with one hand as he snapped a blow to the ulnar nerve in Kortze's upper arm. The terrorist groaned as sharp pain rode through his limb and the Walther popped from numb fingers. Ohara then hooked a knee into his stomach.

Kortze gasped, his breath driven from his body. Ohara hurled his opponent into the sedan. The terrorist swung a left hook at the Phoenix warrior's face. Ohara easily avoided the punch and caught Kortze's wrist in his left hand.

Then Ohara used his right arm like a wrecking ball to demolish the Nazi. He smashed Kortze's jaw, then he slashed a *shuto* chop to the terrorist's breastbone, immediately followed by a back fist to the mouth. Finally, he drove an elbow into the Nazi's solar plexus. Kortze moaned, blood and vomit bubbling from his torn lips. Then he fell unconscious to the pavement.

"Keio," Katz called as he hurried around the wrecked vehicles. "Are you all right?"

"Yes," the Japanese assured him, scooping up Kortze's Walther PPK. "And we have a prisoner."

"Good work, Keio," the Israeli said.

Suddenly, a green Volvo station wagon shot around the corner and skidded to a halt behind the taxicab. Car doors popped open and two men emerged, MP-40 Schmeisser submachine guns in their fists. The driver, Otto Schroder, drew a Mauser HSC pistol from his pocket as he opened the door. The commander of the backup team had no intention of taking any chances with the men they had been ordered to terminate.

The hell with keeping a low profile, Schroder thought. A multiple car wreck would attract the Frankfurt *polizei* anyway. There was no point in trying to be subtle now. He gestured to his men and they opened fire.

Ohara and Katz ducked behind the sedan as twin salvos of full-auto 9mm bullets pelted the taxi and the sedan. Projectiles shattered glass and punctured metal. Katz and Ohara crouched low and waited for the chatter of the Schmeissers to ease up.

The Japanese peeked over the hood of the car. One of the Nazi machine gunners was advancing while the other gunman covered his partner. Ohara glanced at Katz and pointed toward the backup gunman. The Israeli nodded.

"Nein, kameraden," he cried. "Don't shoot."

The terrorists froze, wondering if they were shooting at one of their own men. Ohara quickly aimed the Walther at the nearest gunman and squeezed the trigger. A .380 bullet struck the Nazi in the chest and smashed his sternum. The terrorist staggered and his head jerked backward. The silenced PPK rasped again and another metal messenger of destruction sliced into the hollow of the man's throat.

The Nazi dropped his MP-40 and grabbed his throat with both hands. He fell to his knees, his mouth opening and closing like a ventriloquist's dummy. Blood flowed from his lips and the only sound he uttered was a liquid gurgle of death.

Ohara immediately ducked behind the shelter of the sedan after sending the terrorist to hell. The second machine gunner opened fire at his position. The Japanese tossed the Walther to Katz, who deftly caught it with a steady left hand.

Moving in a low crouch, the Israeli scrambled around the rear of the car and located the second Schmeisser-wielding goon. The terrorist's attention was still on Ohara's position, so Katz could afford an extra half second as he took aim. He braced the Walther across his prosthetic arm, using it as a bench rest.

Shooting to wound, Katz squeezed the trigger. The Walther uttered a metallic belch. The terrorist cried out, dropped his Schmeisser and spun about. His left hand clawed at his right elbow. The joint had been shattered by a well-placed .380 round.

Katz fired another bullet into the terrorist's lower body. The Israeli aimed at the man's right thigh and the .380 dutifully drilled through skin and muscles in the Nazi's upper leg, splintering femur bone beneath. The terrorist hit the pavement, too dazed to do anything except moan and curse through clenched teeth.

Otto Schroder thumbed off the safety of his Mauser and snapped two shots at Katz. Both 7.65mm rounds struck the frame of the sedan. Schroder had no wish to be another victim of the two devil-fighters. Die for the cause? *Donnerwetter nochmals.* The SS had fled after the fall of the Third Reich. Why should Schroder do otherwise?

He slid behind the wheel of the Volvo. Keio bolted from cover and dived for the MP-40 discarded by the dead terrorist. Schroder stomped on the gas pedal. Ohara seized the Schmeisser, executed a shoulder roll and landed on one knee, submachine gun pointing at the Volvo.

Ohara opened fire, exhausting the MP—40 magazine. Bullets punched through the rear window of the car. Two 9mm slugs nailed Otto Schroder in the back of the neck. The Nazi's spinal cord snapped. His body convulsed, fists twisting the steering wheel abruptly to the right.

The Volvo swerved off the road and onto the

sidewalk. It hurtled toward a post office and nose-dived into a brick wall. Stone burst from the building. Metal crushed like cardboard. Schroder was flung through the windshield by the impact. His body slammed into the wall and fell across the crumpled body of the car. Blood trickled from the glass-shredded, broken corpse like a ruptured jug of red wine.

13

General Lieter escorted Yakov Katzenelenbogen and Keio Ohara through the corridors of the BND headquarters building to his office. The other three members of Phoenix Force and Colonel Arness were waiting for them.

"I hear you chaps had a bloody surprise party in Frankfurt," David McCarter said, obviously glad to see his teammates alive and well.

"It was quite a surprise," the Israeli admitted, "but not much of a party.... My hunch has been confirmed."

"Tell us what you came up with," Rafael Encizo said, "and we'll share our news."

"Very well," Katz agreed.

The Israeli explained about the visit to Solomon Wienberg. "And since we were followed and attacked because we saw Solomon," he concluded, "I'd say that's solid evidence that ODESSA is involved."

"Nazis operating with former Baader-Meinhof members?" Arness was stunned. "It doesn't make sense."

"Why not?" Manning inquired. "After World War II a hell of a lot of Nazis and Slavic fascists who found themselves behind the iron curtain simply joined the Communist party. They wound up having the same sort of jobs with Stalin they'd formerly had under Hitler.''

"Colonel Moammar Khaddafi is another example,'' Katz said. "He financed neo-Nazi organizations for years, yet ever since 1973 he's been holding hands with Moscow and supporting leftist terrorists and Marxist groups all over the world.''

"Fanatics can justify anything,'' Ohara said.

"What really concerns us is that we're finally making some headway,'' McCarter declared. "And you managed to capture two live terrorists.''

"That's right,'' General Lieter confirmed. "When I convinced the Frankfurt police to release Herr Katz and Herr Ohara, I also got them to turn over one of the Nazis to BND. The other surviving terrorist is being treated for two bullet wounds. We should be able to question him in another day or two.''

"We may not have another day or two to wait,'' Encizo commented. "When can we question the *bastardo* you brought here?''

"He's being prepared,'' Lieter replied. "Our people have taken blood samples in order to get an estimate as to his physical condition before any truth serums will be used.''

"Well, we think we know where the terrorists will strike,'' Arness declared. "At the NATO 222 missile site.''

''Oh?'' Katz said, raising his eyebrows. ''How did you come to this conclusion?''

''Gary had a stroke of genius,'' McCarter said, grinning. ''I guess it can happen to anyone.''

''Colonel O'Connor and some other officers were killed last night,'' Manning began. ''All were NATO Security personnel, but none of their ID was taken. Then I remembered that the two MPs who had been killed before were attached to the NATO forces.''

''So I ran a check,'' Arness supplied. ''I found that the MPs *had* been with NATO Security and they'd been issued badges identical to the type worn by officers with a NATO Security clearance, except the enlisted men have orange badges and the officers' badges are blue.''

''So the terrorists simply had to photograph the officers' badges in detail in order to have forgeries made based on the MPs' badges already in their possession,'' Katz deduced. ''That way they wouldn't have to draw suspicion by taking the blue badges from the officers' homes.''

''Yeah,'' Encizo said. ''And fake military ID cards could be made based on the real ones taken from the terrorists' previous victims.''

''And, of course,'' Ohara added, ''they will need the Army vehicles to make the charade convincing when they attempt to penetrate the NATO site.''

''The only thing that doesn't fit is ODESSA,''

McCarter said. "If the Baader-Meinhof gang was acting alone, I'd say the KGB was pulling their strings as usual and planned to send them into the missile base to sabotage it. But why would the Nazis get involved in something like this? What the hell would they stand to gain?"

"We were all pretty happy that we'd solved the mystery until you had to open your mouth, David," the Cuban muttered.

"Let's see if our prisoner can answer that question," Lieter suggested.

RUDOLF KORTZE WAS STRAPPED to a chair in a soundproof room. His shirt had been removed and wires were attached to his arms and chest, linking the terrorist to a polygraph machine. Two BND operatives dressed in white lab smocks checked a cardiograph and watched for other possible physical problems.

General Lieter, Gary Manning and Yakov Katzenelenbogen—the two members of Phoenix Force who spoke fluent German—entered the room. Lieter approached Dr. Victor Hahn, head of the BND Medical Section.

"How is our patient, *Herr Doktor*?"

"He's definitely under the influence of the scopolamine," Hahn replied. "I doubt he'll be able to even try to lie in his condition, but if he does, the polygraph will detect it."

"*Sehr gut.*" Lieter nodded. He turned to Katz and Manning. "Go ahead."

Manning looked at Kortze. The terrorist's eyes were closed, his head bowed. He had tried to resist the effects of the scopolamine. A film of perspiration coated his face and torso.

"Wer sind Sie?" Manning asked.

"Ich bin Rudolf Kortze," the terrorist replied in a feeble voice.

"Listen to me, Rudolf," the Canadian said. "You belong to ODESSA, *ja*?"

"ODESSA... *ja*."

"Where is your headquarters located?"

"Brazil...Paraguay...many places. More than one headquarters...strongholds everywhere...."

"Where is the headquarters in Germany, Rudolf?"

"That...that is secret...." Kortze said, shaking his head.

"Tell me, Rudolf. You *must* tell me."

"Nürnberg..." Kortze muttered. *"Nein.* Not Nürnberg. It is...Fürth...."

"He told the truth the first time," Dr. Hahn said, watching the polygraph.

Katz stepped forward. "It is in Nürnberg, Rudolf," he said. "We know that. Where in Nürnberg?"

"Toy factory..." Kortze answered dully. "Konners found it...old abandoned place. Geissler Toy Factory."

"Konners?" Lieter remarked. "That must be Norbert and Helga Konner of the old Baader-

Meinhof gang. We thought they'd fled the country nine years ago."

"Let's talk about that later, General," Manning urged.

"Rudolf," Katz spoke to the prisoner. "The others, your *kameraden*, are there?"

"*Ja* . . . Colonel Müller . . . the others . . ." Kortze replied. "Gunther is dead. . . . Jew shot him. . . ."

"Don't think about that, Rudolf," Katz said gently. "It doesn't matter now. What about the missile site? Tell me about the missiles."

"For Germany," Kortze replied. "Germany reunited . . . one country . . . no more Americans . . . no Russians. . . ."

"With the missiles?"

"*Ja,*" Kortze nodded. "*Die Schweinehunden* leave or we kill them all."

"Rudolf," Katz continued, "when will they go to the missile base?"

"I do not know."

"Tell me, Rudolf. . . ."

"The polygraph needle isn't jumping," Dr. Hahn said. "He's telling the truth. He doesn't know."

"He has already told us enough," Lieter said. "They plan to seize control of the base and use the missiles to try and blackmail the Americans and the Russians into withdrawing their troops from both West and East Germany."

"Yeah," Manning commented, "and there

are people on *both* sides who'd like to see it happen.''

"Perhaps," Katz said, "but neither side would agree to their demands.''

"Do you think they can actually succeed at overpowering a NATO missile base?" Lieter asked.

"I wouldn't dismiss the possibility," Katz replied. "They must also have personnel trained to fire the missiles. ODESSA wouldn't be part of this unless they had a way to make good their threats.''

"Jesus," Gary Manning said. "The Russian, American and NATO Defense missiles are largely computerized to respond immediately to an enemy attack. If those lunatics manage to launch *one* missile in either direction, they could trigger a nuclear war before anybody realized what had happened.''

"That means we'd better hit that damn toy factory before they can make their move," Katz said.

"Right," the Canadian agreed. "Any idea who this Colonel Müller is?''

"Probably some junior SS officer who received promotions from ODESSA since World War II," Katz said. "Whoever he is, we'd better see to his retirement—and make sure it's permanent.''

14

"Our hour of victory is at hand," Heinrich
Müller declared proudly. "Today will go down
in history as the beginning of a new Germany."

He addressed twenty-six men and five women
who had assembled in a large room, formerly
the Geissler Toy Factory's production center.
Müller proudly surveyed his troops.

The terrorists were dressed in American Army
fatigue uniforms, purchased from pawnshops
and through mail-order houses.

"We have planned for this day for many
years," he continued. "I don't need to remind
you of the planning, labor and sacrifice required
to make this day possible. *You* have shared
these hardships. Many of you have waited all
your lives for this day. Now, at last, it has arrived."

Because the Konners and nine other former
members of the Baader-Meinhof gang were included in the assault force, Müller had prepared
his speech for their benefit, also.

"For those of you who have suffered under
the yoke of the imperialist Americans, the revo-

lution you have longed for will finally become a reality.''

Müller noticed several of the terrorists puffed out their chests with pride. He could understand why the Soviets had used the Baader-Meinhof gang—their members were filled with a desire for violence that they tried to justify by claims of idealistic politics.

And that was exactly why Müller intended to dispose of the former Baader-Meinhof members. They were too pliable, too easily manipulated. Revolution was in their blood. Müller did not intend to give them an opportunity to rebel against him.

''Personally,'' the ODESSA colonel said, ''I have but one regret this day. That is that I will not be able to actually participate in the assault. Nonetheless, I shall be with you all in spirit. Now, Herr Konner will give you a final briefing.''

Norbert Konner, clad in fatigue uniform with captain's bars tacked to his collar, stepped in front of the assault team. The terrorist had recently shaved off his beard and mustache, leaving his lower face strikingly pale.

Konner glanced at Helga. She also wore a U.S. Army uniform, her hair clipped short and tucked under her cap. Helga wanted to try to talk the others out of the raid, which she considered an exercise in mass suicide, but she realized such an attempt would be hopeless.

She tried to give her husband a reassuring smile, but her sorrowful eyes betrayed her fears.

"All of you are aware that our ultimate goal is to drive the Americans and Russians out of Germany and establish a single united country under a single government," Konner said. "However, few of you know exactly how this will be accomplished. Of course, security had to be maintained until the last minute— now.

"To be honest, we've been forced to move ahead of schedule. I'm sure you all know everything has gone well until quite recently. Five of our comrades were killed during the last truck hijack attempt, and four more of our people were captured or killed in Frankfurt this morning.

"Those of us who were formerly with the Baader-Meinhof Gang realize the police and the federal forces of the Federal Republic are a highly efficient and formidable enemy. Those of you from ODESSA have no doubt been told that it is a dangerous mistake to underestimate the West German authorities or the Americans. Colonel Müller certainly recalls what the Americans did during World War II. We cannot afford to give our adversaries time to counteract us. We cannot afford to wait."

Heinrich Müller was furious with Konner. Damn fool, the Nazi thought. A commander does not discuss failures or emphasize the competence of the enemy to troops about to be sent on a mission. The bookworm was in danger of demoralizing the strike force before they even left the building. Müller wished Rudolf Kortze had returned from Frankfurt to lead the mission as had been planned.

"The NATO missile site is located here," Müller said, as he marched to a wall map and jabbed a wooden pointer at the target area. "Near the Czech border. The base is over six miles in diameter, but most of that area consists of roads and forests. There are approximately 150 American soldiers stationed at NATO 222, but don't let that worry you. The section you'll be concerned with is Bravo Ten, which is the control center for missile silos twelve to eighteen. There are less than a dozen soldiers on duty there."

"After we've seized control of the silos," Konner interrupted, not about to let the Nazi steal his thunder, "those of you trained to operate missiles will alter their programmed target patterns, aiming them at Munich, Frankfurt, Nürnberg and Bonn in West Germany and Berlin and Leizburg in East Germany. We will then be ready to make our demands."

"Then the occupational forces will be forced to leave and allow us to reunite Germany at last," Müller added.

"And if they refuse," Konner said grimly, "we'll have to use the missiles."

"Ja," Müller nodded. "We will either reunite Germany or destroy her."

HEINZ RITTER slipped into a telephone booth across the street from the Geissler Toy Factory. He hastily inserted two coins into the slot and dialed a number. A familiar voice answered the phone.

"I haven't much time," Ritter said, "the Nazis are sending us out to seize a NATO missile site. . . ."

"You fool," the SSD agent known as Herman replied, stunned by Ritter's disregard for security.

"This is no time to be worried about BND wiretaps," Ritter declared. "It doesn't matter if they are listening. I hope they are. In fact, you'd better contact BND and tell them what ODESSA is planning to do. Contact the Americans too. . . ."

"Give assistance to the enemies of our country?" Herman gasped. "That's treason."

"Damn it," Ritter snapped. "The Nazis *are* our enemies. They've got to be stopped and it doesn't make a damn bit of difference who stops them. If the terrorists get control of those missiles our country will be in as much danger as the Federal Republic."

"Calm yourself, comrade," Herman urged. "I had planned to contact you to give you new orders, but it seems I must do so now."

"What new orders?" Ritter asked. "Can't you see that this changes everything?"

"Nothing overrules your orders," Herman told him. "Our superiors have already guessed that the terrorists planned to use nuclear missiles. Why else would they have taken you and several others trained in the use of these weapons for the mission?"

"So they have a crystal ball in the intelligence department headquarters," Ritter said sourly. "What do they expect me to do now?"

"They seem to see this as a possible blessing in disguise."

"A blessing?" Ritter said in astonishment. "Who regards this as a damned blessing? Is this nonsense coming from the SSD or the KGB?"

"We both know who really runs the German Democratic Republic," Herman said, sighing.

"So the orders come from that pig, General Belmiv," Ritter said, referring to the KGB commander in charge of controlling the SSD for the Kremlin.

"Just listen, comrade," Herman insisted. "The current West German government has been highly critical of the Soviets and very friendly toward the Americans. This is because the parliament of the Federal Republic is an extension of the Yankee imperialists. This is viewed as a greater threat to us than any plot conjured up by ODESSA...."

"That sounds like propaganda for *Neues Deutschland* or *Pravda*," Ritter muttered. "I'm talking about a threat to Germany, not Belmiv's precious Mother Russia. Doesn't Herr Wolf outrank Belmiv? Certainly he would not see this as a blessing.''

"I don't know if Wolf is even aware of this matter," Herman replied. "All I do is follow orders. And all you have to do is follow orders as well.''

"What does Belmiv want me to do?'' Ritter asked, certain he would not like the answer.

"You must, of course, protect the Democratic Republic,'' Herman said. "That means you must not allow the terrorists to fire missiles at our country.''

"How am I supposed to do that, Herman?''

"You'll have to deal with the situation as best you can. However, Belmiv feels it would be agreeable if one or two West German cities suffered from misuse of American NATO weaponry.''

"Agreeable?'' Ritter could not believe what he had just heard. "Agreeable for whom? For what purpose?''

"To undermine the enemies of international communism.''

"Belmiv is willing to kill thousands of innocent people so we can criticize the NATO defense system?'' Ritter was stunned that even the KGB would endorse such a ruthless plan. "That isn't protecting our country from capitalist warmongers. It is utter madness. Belmiv is no better than the Nazis, damn his Russian pig soul.''

"You've got your orders, comrade," Herman stated. "Carry them out as best you can. Good luck."

Herman abruptly hung up. Ritter listened to the monotonous buzz of the dead line in his ear. Good luck, he thought. *Ja,* we will all need luck. Good luck to the entire world.

He slammed the receiver into the phone cradle.

"And may God forgive us all," Ritter whispered.

15

Heinrich Müller pulled the black service cap onto his head and looked at a mirror. Silver SS insignia adorned the lapels of his tunic and a swastika was engraved on every button and on the bronze belt buckle concealed by the black jacket.

General Zeigler had personally given Müller the uniform ten years earlier to commemorate his promotion to *Standartenführer* in ODESSA. It was his proudest possession. Müller wished he could have worn it when he addressed the troops before sending them on the mission, but the Marxist-oriented former Baader-Meinhof members would have been offended.

Perhaps when victory was secured, he and the other Nazis would put on their Party uniforms and celebrate as they did in the old days. Once again there would be parades with bands playing martial music as soldiers goose-stepped through the streets, jackboots slapping cobblestones in rhythm.

The glory of the Third Reich is buried, Müller thought. But ODESSA will resurrect it once again. It would not be the same, of course. Too much had changed over the years. The senior members of ODESSA were old. Most wished only to return to their homeland to die in peace. This time there would be no lunatic leader to lead Germany into war against the rest of the world. They would simply reclaim and reunite their country so the honored old guard of the Nazi party could be safe in their own land.

Nein, Müller thought as he smiled at the reflection in the mirror. We will not attempt to conquer the world. . . .

Not until we are strong enough to succeed.

A KRUMBACHER SHARK LMY-17 gunship flew over Nürnberg. The passengers inside the cabin of the helicopter were the five superwarriors of Phoenix Force.

"There it is," Lieutenant Mertz, the GSG-Nine commando who piloted the gunship, declared. "The Geissler Toy Factory."

"What about civilians in the area?" Gary Manning asked, as he worked the slide of his Wildey autopistol to chamber the first 9mm Winchester Magnum round.

"The local *polizei* helped us evacuate everyone within a city block of the factory," Mertz replied. "There are roadblocks set up to keep people from wandering into the area until we're finished here."

"Do the people have any idea what's going on?" Yakov Katzenelenbogen inquired, checking a Sig-Sauer P-226 pistol before shoving it into a shoulder holster.

"The public has been informed that GSG-Nine is going to hit a terrorist stronghold," Mertz answered. "My countrymen tend to co-operate with the police and GSG-Nine. Of course, we did not tell them about you gentle-men or that ODESSA agents are among the ter-rorists. If they knew about the Nazis, they'd probably tear the building apart before we could stop them."

"The terrorists may well have noticed that the police have cleared the streets," Keio Ohara commented grimly. "They may have prepared a reception for us by now."

"We'll know in another minute or so," Man-ning remarked, gathering up an odd weapon that resembled a *Star Wars* version of a flare pistol. He broke it open and inserted a 40mm cartridge grenade.

The Shark hovered over the factory and Ohara's prediction proved to be accurate. Four men armed with H&K assault rifles poured from the door casing of a garret on the roof. They im-mediately aimed their weapons at the helicopter and opened fire.

Mertz barely glanced at the situation display indicators on the control panel as he moved the copter around to give the terrorists a tougher target. He knew his fighting machine well enough to be certain of his target area at such close range. The pilot pressed the fire button and two machine guns mounted to the main undercarriage erupted. Twin flames spit 7.62mm death at the enemy gunmen.

The terrorists convulsed as the rapid-fire slugs crashed into their bodies. Three German hoods fell to the rooftop, their limbs twitching feebly in death. The fourth man limped to the door of the garret.

Gary Manning slid the cabin door open, aimed his H&K 69A1 at the garret door and squeezed the trigger. The grenade launcher uttered a deep-throated cough and recoiled like a sawed-off 10-gauge shotgun in the Canadian's grasp. A 40mm projectile sailed into the roof. The high-explosive round exploded, ripping the garret apart. Chunks of concrete and wood spewed into the sky. Bloodied remnants of the terrorist were included among the debris.

The chopper moved closer until it hovered over the lip of the roof, nearly touching the surface. Keio Ohara jumped from the gunship, followed by Manning, who grabbed an MP 5A2 submachine gun. Katz, McCarter and Encizo were behind the Canadian.

Another terrorist appeared at the jagged door casing of the shattered garret. The man began to thrust an MP-40 at the five-man army. Ohara was faster. The warrior from Nippon opened fire with an MP 5A2, stamping a column of bullet holes in the Nazi gunman's chest. The terrorist tumbled backward out of sight.

"Stand clear," McCarter shouted, as he pulled the pin from a concussion grenade.

The other members of Phoenix Force parted to give the Briton a clear target. McCarter lobbed the SAS stun bomb through the garret entrance. Dust and rubble belched from the opening.

The five legionnaires of justice charged through the crumbling entrance. Inside the garret, they found a narrow metal stairwell, littered with chunks of debris and the bodies of two terrorists. Rafael Encizo hosed the motionless figures with his MP-5 machine pistol. The volley of 9mm slugs chopped into the enemy troops and sent their corpses rolling down the stairs to a wide catwalk below.

"They were already dead," Manning said.

"Now we can be sure of that," Encizo replied.

The layout of the Geissler Toy Factory was simple and practical. The first floor consisted of the assembly section and a storage area. The second story had two offices and a lunchroom and restroom with the catwalk running alongside the doors.

The terrorists had turned the packing area into a barracks. A diesel-fueled generator powered a series of light bulbs strung throughout the building, and a battery-operated long-range field radio allowed the terrorists to keep contact with agents in the field.

It was far from the most sophisticated enemy

stronghold Phoenix Force had encountered, but it was a hardsite that offered the five warriors little cover when they descended the stairs from the garret to the catwalk.

Fortunately for Phoenix Force, none of the terrorists was prepared for their sudden arrival from the roof—they expected the police to hit the place from the street. Most were stationed at the windows watching for invaders. Others were busy issuing and donning gas masks, assuming the cops would launch tear gas into the factory. Only two ODESSA flunkies positioned on the catwalk saw the five-man strike team descend the stairs. They quickly swung their Schmeissers at Phoenix Force.

Encizo's MP-5 snarled before either Nazi could trigger a weapon. A trio of 9mm rounds stitched the closest terrorist from navel to throat. Another burst of copper-jacketed projectiles from Manning's Heckler & Koch blaster transformed the other ODESSA gunman's face and skull into a spray of red and gray slime.

Another human louse with a swastika for a soul appeared through the doorway of the lunchroom at the opposite end of the catwalk. He prepared to throw a pipe grenade, modeled after an old World-War-II "potato masher." The young Nazi cocked his arm back as Katzenelenbogen's Uzi blasted a stream of rapid-fire parabellums at the man. The ODESSA goon screamed and dropped the grenade as the slugs ripped his right arm from his shoulder and punctured his windpipe.

The potato masher rolled over the edge of the catwalk and fell to the first floor below— much to the horror of two Schmeisser-packing terrorists who were trying to take out Phoenix Force. One man turned to run. The other grabbed the grenade and desperately tried to hurl it at a window. The grenade exploded as it left his fingers, blasting the terrorists into gory chunks.

Three barbarians dashed for the stairs leading to the catwalk, while two others aimed full-auto weapons at Phoenix Force. Katz and Encizo replied with their sub-guns and axed out the pair of ODESSA robots. McCarter blasted a volley of Ingram slugs at the trio on the stairs. Two fell, blood spurting from their bullet-slashed faces and necks. The third retreated only to receive a 3-round burst of 9mm destruction between his shoulder blades.

Manning and Ohara pulled the pins from a pair of M-26 frag grenades. They hurled the hand bombs over the rail of the catwalk as terrorists scrambled across the assembly section, seeking whatever cover might be available. Explosions filled the first floor with white and red glare. Bunks were twisted into mangled metal and scattered across the floor. Shrapnel sliced into flesh and sent dismembered limbs hurtling in all directions.

David McCarter was the first to charge down

the stairs to the first floor, orange hellfire blazing from his M-10. Manning followed while Encizo and Ohara supplied cover fire. The Israeli caught a movement out of the corner of his eye and spun in time to see another terrorist emerging from the lunchroom with an H&K 91 assault rifle in his fists.

Katz squeezed the trigger of his Uzi and blew away the Baader-Meinhof man. The Israeli rapidly yanked the spent magazine from his submachine gun and reached for a replacement from his belt, while Ohara continued to fire at the terrorists below, giving Encizo ample cover as the Cuban dashed down the stairs to join McCarter and Manning.

Suddenly, before the Israeli could finish reloading his Uzi, a door behind him burst open. Two young ODESSA agents exited from the restroom and boldly attacked. One man was armed with a switchblade knife. His bearlike partner had only his bare hands and a lot of muscle, but he was still confident that would be enough to deal with Keio Ohara.

The Israeli raised his empty Uzi in time to block the knife-artist's blade, but the terrorist was fast enough to whip a left hook into Katz's jaw. Both men fell against the handrail. The Uzi and the switchblade were jarred from their owners' fingers and fell to the concrete floor of the assembly section twelve feet below.

Powerful hands seized Katz's throat and a knee crashed into his belly. The younger man snarled as he tightened his grip, determined to strangle Katz to death.

Bright lights seemed to explode inside Katz's head. The terrorist's fingers dug into the Israeli's throat, thumbs jammed deep into his windpipe. The German fanatic was younger and stronger than Katz. He would throttle the Phoenix Force commander in a matter of seconds unless Katz did something fast and did it right.

The Israeli's prosthetic arm snaked out and he clamped the steel hooks around the terrorist's left wrist. With an adroit twist, the steel appendage snapped bone as easily as one might break a pencil in two. The terrorist howled. Katz's left hand quickly *shuto*-chopped his opponent's other arm inside the elbow joint to further weaken the stranglehold.

Katz broke free of his adversary's death grip and smashed the metal hook into the side of the terrorist's skull. The young killer began to sag, but Katz was not finished yet. He grabbed the man's right wrist and pivoted, wrapping the prosthetic arm around the terrorist's captive limb.

The Israeli pulled the man's armpit onto his shoulder and bent his knees for leverage as he hauled the Nazi onto his back. Katz suddenly straightened his legs and arched his spine, sending the terrorist hurtling head over heels. The man screamed as he sailed beyond the handrail and plunged to the deadly concrete below.

Keio Ohara had also been caught off guard. The Japanese spun to confront the Nazi, but the terrorist kicked the gun from Ohara's grasp. The German followed with a solid punch to Ohara's face that propelled Keio into the rail.

With a shout of victory, the ODESSA muscle boy reached for Ohara, planning to toss the Japanese over the side like a bag of dirty laundry. However, Keio Ohara was a twentieth-century samurai commando, as tough as a dragon and as fierce as a tiger, and he never said die.

Ohara grabbed the rail for a brace and swung a roundhouse kick into the brute's left arm. The blow lowered the terrorist's hands. Ohara's foot seemed to deflect off the German's arm and into his face. The terrorist's head recoiled, blood squirting from his broken nose as he staggered backward. Ohara followed him, hopping on his other foot, driving another kick to the man's battered face.

Startled and stunned by the flurry of karate kicks, the terrorist did not react fast enough to prevent Ohara from whipping a knee to his groin. He doubled up with a groan. The Japanese warrior grabbed the man's shoulder with one hand and the back of his head with the other. Then he pivoted and shoved the terrorist's chin over the edge of the rail. Ohara pushed hard and mashed the Nazi's throat into the handrail, crushing his thyroid cartilage.

DAVID MCCARTER EXCHANGED shots with five terrorists who had found cover behind a counter that once served as a display case for toys. The Briton exhausted the ammunition in his Ingram and ducked behind a pillar support for shelter. McCarter began to swap magazines when a volley of bullets from his right broke off a section of the impost above his head, showering him with chips of concrete and dust.

The Englishman crouched. His heart was racing, but excitement overpowered fear. McCarter thrived on action. He discarded the empty M-10 and yanked his Browning Hi-Power from shoulder leather. Another blast of enemy rounds smacked into the side of the pillar. The Briton ignored the pebble-sized debris that dropped on his head. He spotted the muzzle-flash of the sniper's weapon. A former Baader-Meinhof gangster was kneeling by the gutted control panel attached to a rusty assembly rack.

McCarter carefully aimed his Browning in a two-handed Weaver's grip and squeezed the trigger. A 9mm bullet smashed into the terrorist's face, splintering a cheekbone. The man's head was blasted backward, an eyeball swung loosely on its optic nerve. McCarter's next shot hit the man under the jaw. The 115-grain slug sliced off the terrorist's tongue and drilled through the roof of his mouth into his brain.

The five goons at the counter saw an opportunity to blast the Phoenix Force-gunman. They opened fire with an assortment of weapons, modern German military arms as well as World War II vintage models, but McCarter had again ducked behind cover. One of the terrorists carelessly leaned over the counter to fire an old Walther P-38.

Gary Manning had rushed across the assembly section to assist his partner. When he saw the Nazi using the counter for a bench rest, he raised his MP 5A2 and blew the terrorist's skull apart with a trio of 9mm rounds.

The survivors behind the counter dropped low. Manning sprayed the front panels of the counter with a volley of submachine-gun rounds. Bullet holes dotted wood and a scream rewarded the Canadian's efforts.

Two terrorists popped up behind the counter and fired at Manning. The Canadian dived to the floor and rolled to a pillar for cover, bullets cracking against concrete inches from his hurtling body.

Unlike McCarter, Gary Manning was not in love with combat. Maybe the Englishman liked to dodge bullets, but Manning found no joy in it. The Canadian lived for accomplishment, not excitement. He was good at what he did because he gave it one hundred percent. Sure, Manning was an expert with explosives and weapons, but he was also a successful businessman and an authority on industrial security.

As bullets hissed around his position, Manning realized he had not thought about Nemtala since their mission in Germany had begun to get hot. The memory of the woman he loved had not dimmed, but the agony of her loss was diminished by the knowledge that she would want him to continue the war against terrorism.

Mourning Nemtala did not benefit anyone. The greatest memorial Manning could give her would be to fight the modern savages.

Manning swung the MP5A2 around the edge of the pier and opened fire. A terrorist's face vanished in a spray of crimson and pink. The two remaining ODESSA agents hastily ducked behind the counter once more.

McCarter quickly scrambled to their position. The Nazis looked up to see the Briton at the edge of the counter. A cold smile of satisfaction crept across McCarter's face as he aimed his Browning and shot one of the terrorists in the forehead. The other ODESSA killer tried to swing his pistol at the Briton. McCarter pumped two rounds through the man's chest. He kicked the gun from the Nazi's hand before a muscle reflex could cause his finger to pull the trigger.

Rafael Encizo found three terrorists trying to escape through a side door into the alley. The Cuban fired a burst of 9mm slugs at the trio. The bullets broke one man's back, two rounds striking the small of his spine and shattering vertebrae. The terrorist crumpled to the floor as his comrades whirled to return fire.

Encizo leaped over the top of an assembly-line column and huddled behind the pedestal of a balustrade. Enemy bullets ricocheted off metal and sang sourly as they flew in a rerouted direction toward the ceiling. The Cuban braced his MP-5 machine pistol over the rail and pre-pared to pull the trigger.

Then he noticed that one of the terrorists was dressed in a black military uniform. Encizo blinked with surprise and wondered if his im-agination was playing tricks with his eyes. The tall silver-haired terrorist was wearing a Nazi SS officer's uniform.

Encizo thought the Nazi leader could be a useful prisoner, privy to information not only about the current terrorist activity in Germany, but about other ODESSA-related operations throughout the world. Encizo wanted to take him alive if possible. He aimed low, hoping to chop the ter-rorists off at the knees. However, when he squeezed the trigger, the Nazi accompanying Müller suddenly dropped to one knee. The Cuban's bullets struck the clod full in the chest.

Encizo's H&K blaster was out of ammuni-tion. Heinrich Müller smiled and swung his MP-40 at the Cuban. Encizo discarded the machine pistol and desperately reached for the H&K VP70Z on his hip. The Nazi pulled the trigger of his Schmeisser.

A dull click was the weapon's only response.

The ancient submachine gun had misfired and Müller did not have time to clear his weapon. The Nazi cursed, tossed the MP-40 aside and reached for the door. Encizo fired a warning shot into the wall above Müller's head. The SS colonel ignored it and shoved the door open.

Encizo sprang over the column and ran after the sinister black figure bolting out the door.

The Cuban carefully approached the door, which Müller had left standing open. Had Müller fled, or was he lying in wait in the alley?

Encizo peered outside. Still no sign of the Nazi. Where is the bastard? he wondered.

Suddenly, the door rushed toward him. The Cuban tried to dodge it, but it slammed into him hard, smashing his back into the jamb. The Heckler & Koch autoloader fell from his fingers. Heinrich Müller's furious face appeared.

The Cuban shoved hard, swinging the door back at the Nazi, but Müller had already moved. His right arm swung, slashing the barrel of his P.08 Luger across Encizo's skull. The Cuban fell to his knees, his head ablaze with pain.

Müller's jackboot lashed out and kicked Encizo in the face. The Cuban toppled on his back, his skull bouncing on the cobblestone pavement in the alley. Through a crimson haze, he stared up at the towering shape of Heinrich Müller.

"You *schaum* have not won," the Nazi declared. "The Reich will triumph in the end. You are too late to stop that."

The Cuban gazed into the muzzle of the Luger. He did not understand the German words uttered by the ODESSA officer, but the meaning of the gun needed no translation.

"My time to die has arrived," Müller stated coolly, "so I may as well take you with me."

16

The grenade rolled into the office. The three terrorists inside scrambled for cover: two dived behind Colonel Müller's desk while the third pressed himself against a wall, hoping a filing cabinet would shield him from the explosion.

They were still cowering, expecting the grenade to erupt like a volcano, when Keio Ohara charged into the office. The Japanese fighting machine shoulder-rolled across the floor and sprawled on his belly in a prone position, his MatchMaster .45 auto held firmly in both hands. One of the ODESSA goons at the desk raised his head to cautiously peek over the top of the furniture. Ohara aimed and triggered his MatchMaster. A 185-grain hollowpoint slug struck the Nazi just below the hairline and blasted off the top of his skull.

The terrorist crouched by the filing cabinet spotted Ohara and thrust his Skorpion machine pistol at the Japanese. He exposed his head and shoulders to Yakov Katzenelenbogen, who was positioned at the doorway, the Sig-Sauer pistol in his left fist braced across his prosthetic arm.

The Israeli squeezed off three rapid shots.

One 9mm round shattered the terrorist's jaw-bone. Another drilled through his left ear and entered the brain. The terrorist did not even feel the third slug, which tore a chunk from his shoulder; he was already dead.

Crouched behind the desk, the final terrorist did not know whether to open fire at Ohara or Katz. He chose instead to lie low and hope his comrades would rescue him. Katz fired at the desk, taking advantage of the impressive ammunition capacity of the P226 autoloader.

He blasted eight rounds into the side of the desk. Wood splintered. Some slugs buried themselves in the wood, but others pierced the panel. Two bullets found human flesh.

The terrorist felt the lead hornets puncture his rib cage. He cried out and recoiled away from the desk. Ohara blasted a .45 bullet into the center of the terrorist's chest as Katz fired two 9mm missiles into his upper torso. The German thug fell into a corner and slumped to the floor.

Keio Ohara gathered up the grenade he had tossed into the room. It had not exploded because the pin had not been pulled from the primer. The Phoenix Force pair wanted to search the office for information about the terrorist operation; thus the grenade had been used only to distract the enemy long enough for Ohara and Katz to launch the genuine attack.

"The shooting has stopped," Ohara remarked.

"See if the others need any help," Katz instructed. "I'll check the office and see what our hosts left us."

The Japanese nodded. He could not read German so he would be of little assistance in searching the terrorist files. Ohara stepped onto the catwalk and saw David McCarter mounting the stairwell, Ingram held ready in his fists.

"You chaps need a hand?" the Briton inquired.

"I was about to ask you the same question," Ohara replied.

"Everything seems under control downstairs," McCarter stated.

"Any prisoners?"

"Nobody asked us to take any," the Englishman said. "Is Rafael with you blokes?"

"No," the Japanese said, frowning. "Did he say he was coming up here?"

"Didn't see him downstairs," McCarter replied tensely. "Shit. Where is he then?"

COLONEL HEINRICH MÜLLER TOWERED over Rafael Encizo, his Luger aimed at the Cuban's chest. Encizo lay sprawled on his back, the S&W Airweight pinned beneath his body. He had access to only one weapon, one chance to strike out at the Nazi leader.

His hand streaked to the shaft of the Gerber Mark 1 jutting from the top of his boot. Müller gasped with surprise when the Cuban suddenly twisted about like a fish thrashing on the shore. The Nazi had thought Encizo was too stunned to move with such speed. Startled, he pulled the trigger.

The Luger roared.

Encizo felt stone split from the pavement when the bullet struck less than an inch from his left elbow. A combat veteran with more than two decades of experience, Encizo channeled the terror of his close brush with death into action.

Encizo's arm became a blur as he hurled the knife at the Nazi. The double-edged blade of the Gerber struck Müller in the stomach. The point pierced skin and muscle, puncturing the abdominal aorta. The Nazi screamed and folded. His arm jerked away from Encizo as he fired the Luger. The second shot was wild, yards off target.

The Cuban immediately rolled on his left side and reached back to grab the butt of the S&W snubnose in a pancake holster near the small of his back. Encizo broke the restraining strap with a flick of his thumb and drew the revolver. He snap-aimed and triggered the Airweight twice, drilling both .38 rounds into Müller's chest.

The Nazi dropped the Luger and fell to his knees, an expression of total astonishment filling his face. Encizo rearranged the SS officer's features with a 125-grain wadcutter slug. Colonel Heinrich Müller sprawled across the alley and landed on the shattered, bloodied mask that had formerly been his face. His body twitched weakly.

"Rafael," Gary Manning called as he appeared at the door. "You okay, *amigo*?"

"Yeah," the Cuban replied. But, when he tried to stand up, the inside of his head swam in circles and he fell on his backside. "Well... maybe I've felt better."

"Take it easy, pal," Manning urged. "The battle is over. We wiped out the bastards. Closest thing to a casualty on our side seems to be you. Congratulations," Manning remarked as he turned the corpse over with his boot. "You fragged Colonel Müller himself. Nice of him to decide to wear his SS uniform so we could recognize the son of a bitch."

"Müller wouldn't put on his fucking Nazi uniform unless he had a reason," the Cuban said as he stood up. "When does a retired military officer don his old duds?"

"Some sort of special occasion," Manning replied.

"Right," Encizo said.

"You think he addressed the troops in uniform before sending them on their mission to hit the NATO site?" Manning asked.

"Probably not," Encizo said. "But would it surprise anyone if a Nazi colonel went up to his room or his office and put on his uniform *after* seeing the strike force off? You know, Nazi pride and glory."

"Good point, Rafael," Manning agreed.

"Bloody hell," David McCarter groaned as he stepped into the alley. "Keio and I have been looking all over the ruddy place for you two. And where do I find you? Standing around psychoanalyzing a dead Nazi.''

"We've got to get to the NATO site pronto," Encizo declared. "The terrorist strike team is probably already on its way there."

"No kidding?" McCarter snorted. "Katz already came to that conclusion. He also found a map of the area with the exact target spot marked. So, if you two are finished playing Sigmund Freud...."

"I THOUGHT you guys were trying to keep a low profile," Colonel Arness commented when he met Phoenix Force at a helicopter port on the roof of the BND headquarters. "That raid on the Geissler factory was televised, for chrissake."

"Congratulations," Colonel Bohler said good-naturedly. "You men could probably get your own television program if you stayed in the Federal Republic."

"This isn't a joking matter, Colonel," Arness said crossly. "That incident at Frankfurt already attracted too much attention. Now, you five wind up in the middle of a special news bulletin. The involvement of a special team of— excuse the expression—mercenaries working for the United States is bound to cause the sort of scandal we don't need."

"We don't like public exposure any more than you do, Colonel," Katz assured him. "But under the circumstances, there was no alternative that would allow us to act quickly enough.''

"Besides," Manning added, "since the streets had to be cleared there was no way to prevent the media finding out. All civilian aircraft were ordered to keep out of the area. No news-copter with a zoom-lens camera hovered close enough to get a clear shot of us when we hit the factory.''

"After we finished with the terrorists," Ohara said, "we returned to the roof. Another helicopter full of Colonel Bohler's commandos had already landed next to our chopper. As we left, two more GSG-Nine gunships were approaching. There would seem to be enough aircraft hovering back and forth to confuse anyone who might be observing us from a distance.''

"I saw a videotape of the news bulletin," Bohler said. "All it shows is the building with helicopters moving over the roof. There is nothing to suggest it was not strictly a GSG-Nine operation.''

"Colonel Arness," Encizo said, "right now, let's concentrate on stopping the goddamn terrorists. Okay?''

"Now, wait a minute," Arness began. "I've cooperated with you men since you arrived. This hasn't been a typical Army Intelligence operation, but I've tried to handle it as well as I could—although I still don't really know who the hell you people are. I'm trying to do a job, the same as you are.''

"We appreciate that, Colonel," Manning assured him. "And we need your help now to stop the terrorists from seizing control of the NATO 222 missile base."

"I'm not certain I can help you this time," Arness admitted. "After all, I'm going to have a hell of a time trying to convince NATO Security that a gang of German terrorists disguised as American GIs are going to try to infiltrate one of their bases. It sounds too damn incredible."

"Don't forget," Katz said, "most of the terrorists we're dealing with are Nazis. They're old hands at espionage and infiltration. And, according to the files I found in Müller's office, ODESSA has an intelligence network that far exceeds anything we would have thought possible for them to accomplish from their secluded headquarters in South American jungles."

"The fact remains that the terrorists are on their way to the missile site," Keio Ohara declared. "And we will not stop them by standing here discussing the matter."

"That's our Keio," Encizo said. "Practical at all times and annoyingly right as usual."

"The first thing we'd better do is contact NATO Security and warn them," Katz advised.

"That isn't so simple," Arness said. "NATO Security has a top secret crypto radio code. I don't have immediate access to it...."

"Can you get it?" McCarter interrupted.

"Yes," Arness replied. "But I might not be able to convince them that a bunch of Nazis disguised as U.S. soldiers are planning to attack a missile base. They might not take it seriously."

"Don't tell them ODESSA is involved," Manning suggested. "Just instruct them to stop and hold *anyone* who tries to get into the base."

"Or do the standard military routine," Encizo said. "Don't tell them shit."

"Except," Ohara added, "stress that no one should be permitted to enter, regardless of whether their ID seems in order."

"Instruct the NATO personnel to simply order the prisoners to disarm and hold them until we arrive," Katz said. "Then we'll handle it."

"How will you determine if they've got the terrorists or genuine GIS?" Arness asked.

"Easy," Manning answered. "They'll be armed with an assortment of German-made firearms, the same as the terrorists we fought in the factory."

"And those blokes at NATO had better be ready for trouble," McCarter warned. "Emphasize that this isn't a bloody drill. If the terrorists are confronted, they'll probably start shooting."

"How are you going to get to the base?" Arness asked.

"Ludwig?" Katz smiled at the GSG-Nine colonel. "Can we borrow Lieutenant Mertz and his copter a while longer?"

"If the lieutenant volunteers," Bohler said. "And I'm sure he will."

"Fine. Well, Colonel Arness, can you get us cleared to fly into the site?" Katz asked.

"Jesus." Arness rolled his eyes. "I'll be glad when this shit is over."

"Hell, Colonel," Encizo said with a grin. "This kind of *shit* is *never* over."

17

How did this happen to us? Helga Konner wondered as she rode beside her husband in the cab of a U.S. Army truck. How did it come to this?

She remembered when she first met Norbert when they were political science students at Nürenberg University. Helga had hoped to become a civics teacher, while Norbert planned a career as a public servant.

Like most young people, they were idealistic and favored romantic liberal notions. The utopian theory of Marxism appealed to them.

Helga and Norbert became close when they joined a student Communist cell. Their fiery political passion was a common bond, which led to a social relationship and eventually courtship and marriage. It also led them into their involvement with the Baader-Meinhof gang.

Helga could not recall how they actually became terrorists, nor could she remember how they had managed to justify robbing banks and killing innocent people.

The people of the Federal Republic of Germany did not want to be liberated—especially by the Baader-Meinhof gang. No one was taken in by the gang's claim that they were revolutionaries fighting for a brave new world; they were regarded as outlaws and terrorists and treated accordingly. With the support of the public, the police and the newly formed GSG-Nine hunted them down.

The terrorist outfit was soon broken. Andreas Baader, Ulrike Meinhof and other gang members took their own lives. Some gang members joined the German Red Army Faction, while others fled the country. The Konners escaped to Switzerland. Helga hoped her husband would realize that their cause had been folly. Yet even when it became public knowledge that Baader-Meinhof had been used by the Russian KGB, Norbert refused to surrender his warped dreams of revolution and a united Germany under a single socialist government.

Norbert Konner turned to a new source of support. He managed to enlist other fugitive members of the gang and eventually made contact with ODESSA. The Nazis had the only covert organization that was independent of the Soviets, yet powerful and wealthy enough to supply the international connections, finances and manpower needed in Konner's scheme to re-unite Germany. Helga was stunned when the Nazis agreed to the scheme.

She secretly wished they had refused.

Helga felt terrified as the convoy of stolen vehicles approached the NATO 222 site. Even if their plan succeeded, she did not trust the

ODESSA agents. Helga tried to ignore her fear. She had no one except Norbert. Her love for him was her only reality. She was determined to stay with him for better or worse.

Until death did them part.

THE CONVOY REACHED the NATO base's first checkpoint. The headlights of their vehicles knifed through the darkness, shining on the steel gate and twin guard shacks. Two MPs, opening the flap holsters on their hips to allow easy access to their Colt 1911A1 pistols, emerged to meet the terrorists. Two other sentries remained at the guard shacks with M-16 assault rifles within easy reach.

"They're expecting trouble," Helga whispered hoarsely to her husband. "They must have found out about us."

"Don't jump to conclusions," Norbert Konner urged. "This is a NATO missile base. Naturally they're more cautious than most army sentries."

Konner heard the metallic clack of a rifle bolt snapping forward to chamber a round—the sound came from the back of the deuce and a half.

The terrorists had tried to prepare for any possible problem and if the sentries tried to detain them, the assault force had more than enough firepower to blow them away. The terrorists would then have to scrap the mission and flee. Everything, all the planning and years of preparation, would be for nothing. Norbert Konner could not endure another major failure. If they were forced to retreat, he vowed he would shove the muzzle of his Makarov pistol into his mouth and pull the trigger.

"Halt and be recognized," one of the MPs ordered.

Franz Burger, an ODESSA agent, climbed out of the lead jeep. Burger was a middle-aged SS officer. Formerly a member of the Hitler Youth Movement, he had been a fanatical Nazi at the age of ten. Young Franz had been one of the first children to be smuggled out of a Nazi stronghold in Paraguay and placed in a foreign country, becoming a "sleeper" agent for ODESSA.

Burger had spent the past thirty-six years of his life in Illinois, where he was adopted by a pair of American National Socialist zealots. They raised him to be a model United States citizen who obeyed all laws and never publicly criticized America or any ethnic group. They taught him to conceal the extremist politics endorsed by the Nazis. Secretly, Franz Burger was totally dedicated to subversion, racism and the glory of the Third Reich.

He was delighted to be chosen for ODESSA's biggest mission. Dressed in an American Army uniform and field jacket, with a black oak leaf on each shoulder, he was about to play a vital role in the operation.

"Lieutenant Colonel Mandel," he gruffly informed the MP, speaking with the American Midwest accent of his adopted parents. "I'm the XO at NATO Two-Forty."

The MP, a young black specialist fourth-class, glanced at the blue security badge pinned to Burger's left breast pocket. He snapped to attention and saluted.

"Yes, sir," the MP said. "May I ask your business here, sir?"

"I have special instructions for the post commander," Burger replied, annoyed that he had to explain anything to a "subhuman" Negro. "A recon report has informed us of a large increase of heavily armed Russian and Czech troops at the border. This could be in preparation for a full-scale invasion, Specialist."

"An invasion?" the MP blurted out. "Er. . . I'll have to contact the OD, sir."

"Let me talk to him as well," Burger insisted. "I have to explain to him that he'll have to maintain radio silence until the post commander has been fully briefed and given the new code and frequency for transmission. The enemy has broken the old code and they're probably listening on the present frequency. That's why I was sent to personally deliver this information. Radio communication beyond this base could endanger our security throughout Western Europe."

"Sweet Jesus," the other MP whispered. "This could be the big one and we're right in the middle of it."

"Goddamn it," Burger snapped. "Are we going to stand out here and wait for the Ivans to ride over us in their tanks?"

"No, sir," the black MP responded. "Please follow me, sir."

Norbert Konner watched the unsuspecting soldier escort Burger to the guard shack. He heard the shuffle of boots in the back of the truck. Konner thought he even detected the whisper of the canvas flap at the rear of the vehicle as a terrorist climbed out. This was probably his imagination—the pulse behind his ear was thumping too loudly for him to be certain of any other sound.

An eternity crawled by. Scant seconds rode on the shell of a snail as Konner waited and watched the guard shack where Burger stood, speaking into a field telephone. The black Sp 4c. and a buck sergeant stood beside the bogus colonel, their faces stiff with tension. At last Burger hung up and turned to face the pair.

They did not see the silencer-equipped Walther PP in his fist until it was too late.

Burger aimed the pistol at the sergeant and put a bullet in the NCO's chest. The Walther hissed again as Burger purposely gut shot the black Sp 4c. The young MP doubled up in agony.

"Nigger filth," the Nazi snarled as he slammed a knee into the wounded man's face.

The MP fell to the floor of the shack. Burger calmly pumped two more rounds into his victim. Almost as an afterthought, he shot the sergeant in the back of the skull to be certain he was dead.

As the Nazi murdered the two MPs, the other sentries also found death. A terrorist gunman at the side of the deuce and a half opened fire with a Heckler & Koch SD2 submachine gun. A sound suppressor muffled the report of the weapon as a volley of slugs shattered a window on the other guard shack and chopped into the torso of the astonished MP stationed within.

The MP sentry standing alone in front of the enemy convoy made a desperate grab for his sidearm. Ricardo Dieter, the ODESSA agent who drove the lead jeep, fired his silenced Mauser before the American could clear leather. He put two 7.65mm rounds into the MP's upper chest. The soldier fell. Dieter bolted from the jeep and ran forward to deliver a third bullet, which he drilled through the base of the man's neck.

Terrorists leaped from the convoy vehicles.

"We did it," Klaus Werner told Konner as he waved a clenched-fist Communist salute at the terrorist leader. "We're going to succeed, comrade. Tonight will be our storming of the Winter Palace, *ja*?"

Konner did not bother to reply. The mission was far from over. He jogged to the guard shack as Franz Burger emerged. The Nazi grinned.

"Did you convince the officer of the day with your story?" Konner demanded.

"*Ja,*" Burger nodded. "They told us to come

ahead immediately. The next guard post will be alerted to let us through. Good service, eh?''

"That means we don't have to kill the men at the next checkpoint," Helga said hopefully as she joined the pair.

"We can't take any chances," Konner told her. "I'm sorry, dear. They all must die."

"Do not let their deaths worry you, Frau Konner." Burger shrugged. "They are Americans, *ja*? I was raised in the United States. Believe me, Americans hate Germans. So, we will kill the Americans."

Lieutenant Mertz piloted the Krumbacher Shark LMY-17 gunship through the night sky. He glanced at David McCarter as the Briton scanned the forest below with a Starlite viewer.

"We're approaching the NATO 222 site," the GSG-Nine chopper jockey announced. "Hope you guys are ready."

"We're always ready for trouble, mate," McCarter assured him. "Say, Lieutenant, where did you learn to speak English so well?"

"Foreign exchange student," Mertz replied. "I went to high school in Denver. Later I took two years of police science and criminal law at Colorado State U. Might have considered getting U.S. citizenship if I wasn't in GSG-Nine. The work is too important to turn my back on it. Besides, this sort of thing gets in your blood. Know what I mean?"

McCarter smiled. "Bloody right, I know."

"You five are damn good," Mertz commented. "The best I've ever seen, but do you think it's wise to hit the terrorists this way? We could go in there with a company of GSG-Nine commandos as well as plenty of Airborne Rangers from the USAEUR forces."

"And we'd alert the terrorists to trouble if they heard a fleet of gunships closing in," Gary Manning told him as he glanced up from a map of the NATO 222 site.

"Well, you guys know what you're doing," Mertz said with a shrug.

"Have any of you located the road yet?" Yakov Katzenelenbogen asked, a trace of urgency in his voice. "The terrorists are no doubt traveling on it to the missile site."

"Not yet, Katz," Manning answered. "If we don't spot them between here and the base we'll land at Bravo Section."

"Don't worry, Yakov," Keio Ohara assured the team commander. "It won't be much longer."

"Something wrong?" Mertz inquired.

"Katz doesn't like to fly," McCarter explained. "Especially bothers him at night for some reason."

"I hate helicopters worst of all," the Israeli admitted. "These things are like giant dragonflies. They hover and bob all over the sky. At least planes just go straight ahead."

"Party's over," Gary Manning announced, "we're approaching the road."

"Get lower for a better look," Katz told Mertz.

The Shark descended. The men of Phoenix Force did not need their infrared viewers. The floodlights mounted over the guard shacks illuminated the area well enough to reveal shattered windows and stains left by blood and brains. No one stirred below.

"It's deserted," Keio Ohara stated. "The terrorists have already passed through here—they beat our alert."

"Follow the road," Katz instructed. "Keep watching for a convoy of military vehicles."

"And be prepared for them to open fire when we move in," McCarter added.

"But don't attack unless they start shooting," Manning warned. "We don't want to blow the hell out of a convoy full of genuine U.S. soldiers."

"Wait until they start shooting?" Mertz frowned. "I just hope the terrorists don't have a grenade or rocket launcher."

"We'll find out when we catch up with them," Encizo replied. "We'll wrap this mission up then—one way or another."

18

The Bravo Section of NATO 222 did not look like a missile base; it was not supposed to. The base had a small mess hall. Billets were simple wooden structures containing little more than bunks, a latrine and shower rooms. Most of the troops were stationed there only for a couple of weeks, serving guard duty before returning to their regular units.

A network of walls, consisting of sandbags piled four feet high, formed a maze throughout the compound. Most of these were concentrated around the main building. Headquarters was no larger than the billets, although it was made of concrete. The most important part of the installation was not visible.

The site's missile control center was buried deep beneath the ground. Six Warhawk missiles were located in subterranean silos.

Inside the headquarters, post commander Captain Willard Long had not been impressed by the report of alleged increases of Russian and Czech troops at the border. Anyone familiar with duty at the DMZ was accustomed to the Soviets' fondness for saber rattling. If the Communists really intended to attack they would either start the fireworks by launching missiles or attempt to slip across the border to take out the NATO defense weapons first. Either way, there would be no point in building up the number of tanks and troops at the Czech border.

Then why was this Colonel Mandel character bringing a convoy into the site? Why had he selected Bravo Section? What the hell was really going on?

The telephone on Long's desk rang. He picked up the receiver, his mind still puzzling over Mandel and the mystery convoy.

"Bravo Section, Captain Long speaking, sir," he spoke into the mouthpiece.

"This is Major Carson," a familiar voice declared.

"Yes, sir," Long replied. Carson was the XO of the headquarters battery of NATO 222.

"I just received a message that a convoy of enemy troops is trying to infiltrate your section, Captain," Carson told him. "I have not been able to get any confirmation on this, but it sounds suspicions as hell."

"It sure does, Major," Long agreed, an icy tremor crawling up his spine.

"I tried to contact the road checkpoints," Carson added. "No one answered."

Long's fist tightened around the telephone handset.

"When that convoy arrives, hold them,"

Carson ordered. "Don't let anyone pull rank on you. I'll take responsibility. A special team of some sort, CIA spooks or something, is being flown in by helicopter to question these people. When they arrive, you're to turn the prisoners over to them. Understood?"

"Yes, sir."

"Captain," Carson added sternly. "Arm your men and tell them to be ready to blast the members of the convoy if they resist."

"Yes, sir," Long said woodenly.

"I'll send reinforcements as soon as possible," Carson promised. "Hang tough, Captain."

The major hung up. Long slapped the receiver into the phone cradle. He yanked open the top drawer of his desk and reached inside for a holstered Colt .45. Long buckled on his gun belt as he strode across the office toward the door. It opened before he reached it.

"Sir," a young Pfc who served as Long's orderly-room clerk began, "the convoy is here, sir."

Long whirled and stared out a window. Four vehicles—two trucks and two jeeps—had just rolled through the front gate into the parade field. Figures clad in U.S. Army fatigues poured from the rigs. They wielded an assortment of weapons, but the captain's attention instantly zeroed in on a man aiming a long tubular device at the office building.

"Holy Christ," Long gasped.

Klaus Werner fired the RPG-7 rocket launcher. Flame spewed from the muzzle of the Soviet-made blaster and a projectile sailed into the front of the headquarters building.

The door of the headshed was blown off its hinges. The offices within were crushed. Captain Long and his clerk were ripped apart before the wreckage buried their corpses.

The soldiers stationed at Bravo Section were caught totally off guard. The terrorists immediately opened fire on the sentries, cutting them down with automatic fire before the defenders could get off a single shot. Other fanatical killers lobbed grenades into the mess hall. The building exploded and collapsed into a pile of smoldering rubble, crushing the men within.

The men in the billets were totally defenseless, since their weapons had been turned in to the arms room at the headshed after their guard shifts ended. Terrorists hurled thermite grenades into both barracks. Flaming liquid exploded, splashing the hapless Americans with burning agony. Thermite ate through clothes and flesh, burning into muscle and bone.

The screaming GIs stumbled from the billets. Perhaps they were suffering too much to realize certain death waited outside—or perhaps they purposefully chose the door because the rapid death by full-auto bullets was better than the living hell of having liquid burn through their tissues. The soldiers charged directly into the path of dozens of flying lead projectiles that smashed the life from their charred bodies.

"The operators of the missiles are below," Konner declared, thrusting the barrel of his Makarov at the remains of the headshed. "Get down there fast. When they realize what's happened, the Americans might try to destroy the control panels."

Half a dozen terrorists dashed to the crumbling entrance of the headquarters building. Konner stayed with the vehicles and ordered the other men to assume positions throughout the base. He sent two sentries to the guard shacks and told them to close the gate. Others moved to the sandbags, while another team was instructed to make certain all the Americans were dead.

The hit team sent to capture the missile control center found their task to be remarkably simple. The steel door leading to the subterranean sector was standing wide open. A pale-faced young trooper stood in the doorway, trying to pull it shut. A burst of Schmeisser 9mm rounds stopped him dead.

Gunmen eagerly crowded through the door, trampling the corpse of the slain technician. Franz Burger was the first to reach the metal staircase that led to the underground nerve center. However, Burger's zeal earned him a .45 slug in the gut. He screamed and plunged head-first down the stairs.

A young warrant officer, stationed behind a control console below, fired his 1911A1 auto-loader at the invaders. A 230-grain solid ball bullet sparked against the steel handrail as the hit team crouched low. They thrust the muzzles of their weapons through the baluster supports.

Volleys of full-auto rounds raked the American's position. The WO1's head snapped back as four bullets nearly ripped it from his neck. The soldier's body collapsed behind the control panel.

"That seems to be all of them," Ricardo Dieter, in charge of the hit team, announced. "Schultz and Ritter, check the consoles for damages. Gurber and I will make certain all these American scum are dead."

The terrorists carefully descended the stairs. Dieter and Rolf Gurber searched the sector while Heinz Ritter checked the motionless form of Franz Burger, who lay at the foot of the stairs, his head turned in an ugly unnatural position.

"There does not appear to be any damage to the controls," Kurtz Schultz stated. His German contained a trace of a Cambridge accent. Schultz had received his training in nuclear missiles from the British Air Force, which never suspected he was an ODESSA sleeper agent.

"Burger is dead," Ritter told the others. "His neck must have been broken when he fell down the stairs."

"One casualty," Dieter said, shrugging.

He waved his MP-40 machine gun at the control panel. "You two know what to do, *ja*?"

"*Ja,*" Schultz said. "We will adjust the coordinates to aim the missiles at new targets. *Our* targets."

"Stay with them, Gurber," Dieter ordered as he headed for the stairs.

"At last the enemies of the Reich will feel our fury," Schultz said.

"If only *der Führer* could be here to see the resurrection of his dream," Gurber added.

Heinz Ritter glanced up the stairs to confirm Dieter had left. "Hitler might be disappointed," he remarked as he turned to face the other two.

Schultz and Gurber stared at Ritter with astonishment. The SSD double agent aimed his Walther P-38 at the pair. The nine-inch silencer attached to the barrel barked softly as a 9mm dumdum slug smashed into Gurber's forehead.

The ODESSA goon collapsed. Schultz fumbled with his side arm and opened his mouth to cry for help. Ritter shot him in the face, drilling a Walther round through the Nazi's left eye socket. The only sound Schultz uttered was a startled gasp as he was hit by death.

Ritter quickly mounted the stairs and pulled the steel door shut. He bolted it, noting the trio of metal latches that snapped into place at the side, top and bottom of the door. Good security. The others would have to blast the door to open it. By then, the SSD agent's work would be complete.

East Germany would be safe.

But a nuclear missile would be on its way to destroy Munich.

19

"Bloody hell," David McCarter muttered as the helicopter approached Bravo Section. "The bastards have already hit the place."

"So now we hit them," Gary Manning stated grimly, gazing through a Starlite viewer at the burning billets in the distance.

"Lieutenant Mertz, let us out here," Katz instructed. "Give us exactly five minutes to get in position and then close in."

"You got it," the GSG-Nine pilot said.

"But don't get too close," Keio Ohara advised. "They must have some sort of rocket launchers to cause so much damage."

"Right," McCarter said, placing a hand on the pilot's shoulder. "We don't want you to get killed, mate. It's a long walk home."

The five men of Phoenix Force decided on a plan of action, then they gathered up their weaponry and slipped on thick leather work gloves. The Shark gunship descended slowly. Encizo and Ohara lowered the hoist cables from the undercarriage while Manning opened the cabin doors.

McCarter swung his long body outside and

seized the closest cable. He swooped over the side and locked his ankles around the cable. The Briton caught the second line and swung it into the eager hands of Keio Ohara. Then McCarter descended, using hands and legs to slide down the first line.

One by one, they followed. Ohara, Manning and Encizo soon joined McCarter on the ground. They gazed up to watch Yakov Katzenelenbogen slither down the cable. The middle-aged amputee descended the line as rapidly and easily as his younger teammates.

"All right," the Israeli said, "you all know what to do. Any questions?"

No one spoke until Encizo piped up: "Let's get on with it."

THE TERRORISTS HEARD the sound of giant propellers slicing through air before they could see the ominous shape of the Krumbacher gunship in the distance. The chopper approached slowly. Norbert Konner ordered Klaus Werner to get the RPG-7 rocket launcher.

"Blast the helicopter," Konner instructed. "Shoot it out of the sky."

"It is not close enough, comrade," Werner replied.

"If it gets much closer it will be able to fire rockets at us," Ricardo Dieter stated.

"But I'll probably miss from this range," Werner insisted.

"Fire anyway," Konner said. "Perhaps it will frighten the helicopter away."

"Or startle the pilot into firing at us," Dieter warned. "Many American gunships are equipped with machine guns and heat-seeking Sparrow missiles."

"Donnerwetter," Konner growled. "I did not think the Americans would react so quickly."

"Maybe it's just a patrol copter," Werner suggested. "It may have seen the fires from the sky."

"Let's try to make radio contact," Helga urged. "Let the pilot return to his base and tell the others that we have control of the missiles and we're ready to use them if we have to."

"Yes," Konner agreed, watching the gunship fly in a wide circle around the base. "Dieter, we need one of your English-speaking comrades."

"The only one left is Schultz," the ODESSA agent replied. "He's with Ritter, altering the programmed targets of the missiles."

"Get him," Konner ordered. "Klaus, keep that rocket launcher ready in case...."

The sudden bellow of an explosion at the west wing of the compound startled the terrorists. Werner panicked and triggered the RPG-7. He fired the weapon at the helicopter, unaware that the gunship had not launched the attack on the base. The Russian rocket launcher spit a HE projectile toward the chopper, but the rocket lost momentum and plunged to earth before it reached its target.

"You fool," Konner snapped. "The attack came from over there."

He pointed to the west as more explosions erupted from other directions. The gate was ripped and hurled inside the compound. Two terrorists stationed at the entrance bolted and ran a few yards before they fell on their bellies; they had been hit by a spray of 9mm rounds from a silenced MP 5A2 submachine gun.

Fence sections and shrapnel sliced through the air, bombarding the terrorists. Konner shouted commands to his men as he tried to set up a defense against the invaders.

The former members of the Baader-Meinhof gang were less disciplined than the ODESSA agents, who had been raised in a militaristic environment since birth. The Nazis did not need Konner's advice. They had already rushed to the sandbags for cover, aiming their weapons at the tattered holes in the fences.

Then Lieutenant Mertz unleashed an aerial torpedo. It sizzled from the undercarriage of the Shark and streaked through the night sky like a miniature comet. The rocket struck one of the enemy trucks. The deuce and a half exploded in a shower of flaming debris, sharp jagged metal and chunks of human flesh that had once been terrorists.

As the truck exploded—while the terrorists were ducking for their lives—Phoenix Force charged into the compound. Ohara and Encizo dashed through the shattered gate. Katz and McCarter hit the enemy from the east. Manning attacked from the west.

The Canadian aimed his H & K 69A1 at the sandbag barrier and blasted a 40mm grenade into a nest of German barbarians. A brilliant glare blossomed from the section as the burst of HE transformed the barricade into a shower of loose sand, torn burlap and mangled corpses. Four ODESSA agents were blasted hellbound.

The dead bodies were hurled against one of their comrades. The corpses served as a shield and protected the man, who was bowled over and buried under the dead men, his weapon knocked from his hands.

The terrorist looked up and saw Manning charging through the opening created by the H & K 69. The Canadian had slung the grenade launcher over his left shoulder and now held an MP 5A2 in his fists. The only weapon the Nazi could reach was a bayonet on his web belt.

Only a lunatic would consider attacking a man armed with a submachine gun while only armed with a knife. The Nazi was a lunatic, further crazed by desperation. He waited until Manning passed, then pushed his way out from under his slain comrades and attacked the Phoenix Force hellfighter.

Manning sensed the presence of danger and whirled in time to see a blur of motion as the Nazi rushed forward. Before Manning could trigger his weapon, the German dived into him. Both men hit the ground, the ODESSA agent on top, his bayonet poised to strike.

The Canadian raised his MP 5A2 and blocked

the Nazi's attempt at thrust. Quickly, he caught the man's wrist. The ODESSA flunky's free hand clenched into a fist and he smashed Manning in the face. The bitter taste of blood filled Manning's mouth.

The Canadian's legs suddenly snaked out and encircled his adversary's waist. He wrapped them around the Nazi, locked his ankles together and squeezed forcibly. The German gasped as Manning's powerful legs constricted under his ribs. The Canadian twisted his hips and swung his opponent to the side. The Nazi suddenly found himself on his back with Manning on top.

Still exerting pressure with the leg lock and holding the man's wrist to control the bayonet, Manning hammered the bottom of his free hand into the bridge of the Nazi's nose, shattering the nasal cartilage. Blood squirted from the German's nostrils. Manning then drove the heel of his palm under the terrorist's nose. The blow sent splinters of already broken cartilage upward, through the sinus cavity and into the brain.

Yakov Katzenelenbogen located a trio of terrorists cowering behind one of the jeeps. A salvo of Uzi rounds pinned down the cannibals. The Israeli swiftly inserted a prosthetic hook into the ring of an M-26 grenade and pulled the pin. He tossed the death dealer across the pavement; it rolled under the jeep.

Katz threw himself to the ground as the

enemy troops popped up from cover and return- ed fire with full-auto weapons. Bullets burned air above the Israeli's prone body. He clenched his teeth and held his breath, every muscle tight with tension.

Five seconds dragged by. At last the M-26 ex- ploded. The grenade blew both the jeep and the terrorists to pieces. A grisly fallout of torn metal and bloodied flesh rained over the compound.

Two terrorists, using an army truck for cover, moved to the cab in an attempt to retreat from the base. Neither man realized Rafael Encizo had discovered them. Using the base of a guard shack for cover, the Cuban opened fire with his MP-5 SD1 machine pistol.

Nine-millimeter slugs butchered the fanatics. Their bullet-riddled bodies were propelled along the length of the cab by the rapid-fire projec- tiles. Encizo watched the corpses crumple to the ground and he prepared to advance.

Then he glimpsed the dull reflection of gun- metal out of the corner of his eye.

Encizo turned, slashing the barrel of his H&K miniblaster into the Walther PPK that an ODESSA agent had aimed at the Cuban's head. The Walther was knocked from the terrorist's numb fingers. The Nazi reacted with a quick slash with the heel of the palm to Encizo's wrist. The Cuban dropped his machine pistol.

Encizo's reflexes were sharp. He threw a cross-body *shuto* chop into the facial nerve under the Nazi's jaw and stamped a boot heel into the man's instep. The stunned terrorist began to stagger backward, but Encizo quickly grabbed the man's head with both hands. He pivoted, turning his opponent, placing himself back to back with the killer.

Still holding the man's head, Encizo yanked hard, tugging the back of the German's neck across his shoulder. The Cuban suddenly dropped to one knee and pulled the Nazi's head even harder. Vertebrae crunched. Encizo released the terrorist, who slumped to the ground.

David McCarter had plunged into the heart of the battle. The Briton located a lone terrorist positioned at the wall of sandbags. He sliced off the top of the Nazi's skull with a burst of 9mm Ingram slugs and vaulted the barricade, landing feetfirst on the dead man's chest.

Moving along the wall, McCarter almost ran into Klaus Werner and Karin Stoffer, another reject from the Baader-Meinhof gang. Werner had discarded his rocket launcher and armed himself with a M-16 assault rifle he had confiscated from a dead GI. The woman held a Skorpion machine pistol—a favorite weapon of European terrorists. Both swung their guns toward McCarter.

Neither got a chance to unload a single shot.

The Briton's M-10 spat a volley of 115-grain flesh-shredders. The woman's fatigue shirt acquired four bloody holes. Werner received two slugs in the upper torso. The M-16 seemed to hop from the terrorist's hands when the impact kicked him backward over the sandbags.

McCarter advanced, swapping magazines for the M-10. He removed the spent mag and was reaching for a fresh 32-round clip when he saw Werner rising on the summit of the sandbags.

Although his right collarbone was broken and his sternum had been cracked by a bullet, Werner was determined to keep fighting. The fanatic leaped from the wall and threw himself at McCarter.

Bleeding lunatic, McCarter thought. The Briton quickly raised the empty M-10 and smashed the frame into the terrorist's face. The blow propelled Werner back into the sandbags.

"Stupid bastard," McCarter growled as he stepped forward and slashed a boot into the dazed man's groin.

Werner's eyes swelled in agony and blood bubbled from his crushed mouth when he groaned. The Englishman drew his Browning Hi-Power automatic from shoulder leather and snapped off the safety. He thrust the muzzle of the pistol into the German's torn lips and pulled the trigger. The back of Werner's skull exploded, splattering blood and brains across the sandbags. The Briton pulled the Browning from the dead man's mouth and used Werner's shirt to wipe the blood off its frame.

Keio Ohara was the first to reach the entrance to the main building. He slipped inside and found Ricardo Dieter crouched at the doorway, trying to clear a bent cartridge casing from the breech of his Schmeisser. The Japanese pointed the muzzle of his MP 5A2 at the Nazi's face.

"Drop it," Ohara ordered.

Dieter's mouth fell open as he stared up at the tall Oriental. The ODESSA thug slowly raised his arms, the MP-40 still in his fist. Ohara sighed.

"I said *drop it*."

Ohara's right leg swung a lightning-fast reverse-roundhouse kick. The side of his foot smashed into Dieter's hand, sending the Schmeisser flying. The Nazi howled and tried to kick Ohara in the groin.

The Phoenix Force commando sidestepped Dieter's boot and lashed a butt-stroke at the side of the ODESSA man's skull. The Nazi ducked the H&K, seized the frame of the subgun and tried to twist it from Ohara's grasp. The tactic might have worked if Keio Ohara had not been a judo expert.

Moving with the terrorist, Ohara pivoted and placed his hip against the man's midriff. Then he pulled hard, tossing Dieter to the floor. The Nazi landed on his back. Ohara promptly stomped the edge of his foot into Dieter's throat. Blood spewed from the man's lips, spilling crimson on Ohara's boot. With a soft moan the Nazi died.

"Where's the control center?" Katz asked Keio as he stormed into the headshed.

"I just arrived," Ohara replied. "But I suspect it is there."

He pointed his H&K at the steel door at the end of the hall. Both men hurried to it. Katz tried the handle.

"Locked," the Israeli said tensely. "We'll need explosives to open it."

"Gary can do that," Ohara stated.

"But if the terrorists are already inside," Katz said grimly, "they may have already had enough time to sabotage the missiles."

"So if we blow the door," Ohara said, "the terrorists will launch the missiles."

Katz nodded.

"If they haven't already done so."

EPILOGUE

"We've got to get out of here, Norbert," Helga cried.

"Nein," her husband snapped as he pried a MP-40 submachine gun from the lifeless figure of a slain ODESSA agent. "We will fight our way to the control building and buy a few extra minutes for our comrades to complete their mission. The missiles will be launched."

"Mein Gott, Norbert," Helga sobbed. "How are we going to liberate anyone by killing *thousands* of innocent people."

"No one is innocent," Konner replied bitterly. "Now, help me one last time, Helga."

The couple climbed into a jeep. Helga slid behind the steering wheel as her husband positioned himself in the seat next to her, bracing the Schmeisser over the edge of the door. The woman turned on the ignition and stomped the gas pedal to the floor. The vehicle shot forward, rocketing toward the headquarters building.

David McCarter, Gary Manning and Rafael Encizo had dashed to the entrance of the building to join Ohara and Katz. They saw the jeep speed toward them. Norbert Konner fired the MP-40 wildly in all directions while his wife drove, her vision almost obscured by tears.

"Jesus," McCarter gasped. "They think they're bloody kamikaze pilots."

Manning yanked the Wildey autoloader from its holster. He extended his arms, holding the big steel pistol in a Weaver combat grip as he thumbed off the safety. He triggered the weapon three times, his powerful arms absorbing the recoil smoothly.

All three bullets pierced the windshield of the jeep. Helga Konner's face dissolved. Norbert was splashed by the hideous slime that had formerly been his wife's head.

"Helga," he wailed.

The decapitated corpse slumped to the right, hands still locked on the steering wheel. The vehicle swerved violently and sped into a wall of sandbags. It crashed through the top of the barrier and lunged forward.

Norbert Konner was thrown from the vehicle. He hit the ground an instant before the nose of the jeep crashed to earth. The vehicle rolled over the fallen terrorist leader, crushing his body.

Yakov Katzenelenbogen appeared in the doorway. "Manning, we need you to blast open the door to the control center."

Gary Manning placed a few ounces of C-4 plastic explosive into the triple latches of the steel door. He then inserted pencil detonators into the white puttylike substance. The Canadian, Katz and Ohara found cover and waited ten seconds for the C-4 to do its work. The explosion seemed relatively mild, yet the door swung open, the steel latches blown away, the jamb warped by the blast.

Ready for action, the trio charged in.

Death waited below.

Four corpses littered the floor of the control center. A fifth body sat in a chair by one of the consoles. His head was cracked open like a blood-filled eggshell; a Walther P-38 was still gripped in his fist.

"Shot himself," Ohara declared, looking at the powder burns on the dead man's right temple.

"The missiles haven't been fired," Manning said after glancing over the controls. "And they haven't changed any target areas for the missiles either. They couldn't. This system doesn't have the capacity to reverse preprogrammed targets. It would be impossible to launch any of these missiles at cities in West Germany."

"But he still could have fired them at East Germany," Katz remarked, looking down at the corpse of Heinz Ritter. "I wonder why he chose to commit suicide instead of accomplishing that half of his mission."

"He must have had a reason," Manning said wearily. "What the hell. *Our* mission is accomplished. Let's get out of here."

The Gar Wilson Forum

Dear Jack Miller:

My editor forwarded your letter to me, but your address did not include the city and state in the upper right-hand corner. Hopefully, you'll get to read this when you pick up the book. Gold Eagle is a great publishing house. They make copies of all the fan letters and really pay attention to our readers.

Thank you very much for your kind remarks about Phoenix Force. Glad you enjoy the series. I'm also glad you like the character of David McCarter. He is indeed one baad-ass. In future books, you'll get to know McCarter better. There will be more insight into the guy's personality, and you'll get to see what makes McCarter tick.

Okay, to answer a couple of your questions: McCarter is currently thirty-four years old and in excellent health, despite the fact that he smokes a bit too much and picked up that Coca-Cola habit. By the way, David smokes British Players cigarettes.

David McCarter uses a variety of assault rifles, but he tends to favor close-quarters weapons. His favorite weapons are his Browning Hi-Power 9mm pistol and the M-10 machine pistol (he's holding it on the cover of *Dragon's Kill*; in the picture, McCarter has a foot-long silencer attached). The M-10 was developed by Gordon Ingram. It is a dandy weapon with a 32-round capacity that can fire either semi- or full-auto. The M-10 comes in both 9mm and .45-caliber. McCarter naturally uses the 9mm model because it is the same caliber as his Browning.

McCarter is the best pistol shot among the entire Phoenix Force team. He favors an SAS British concussion grenade or an American made M-26 fragmentation grenade, although he isn't really fond of explosives like Gary Manning is. McCarter is also an expert in jujutsu (taught to SAS British commandos) and he learned some Wing-Chuan kung fu while stationed in the Orient. Of course, McCarter is an ace pilot who can fly anything from a glider to a commercial jetliner.

Like you said, a real baaad-ass!

Best wishes always,

Gar

PHOENIX FORCE

AN EXECUTIONER SERIES

#10 Korean Killground

**MORE GREAT ACTION
COMING SOON!**

In a rash of nocturnal border raids, American GIs and other peacekeeping forces were being murdered near the Korean DMZ. All evidence pointed to Communist terrorists.

Phoenix Force landed amid Asian turmoil to probe the atrocities. Twice they crashed the buffer zone, and twice they were suckered. They returned to base scratching their heads: was there a leak in internal security? Who was this phantom enemy?

Finally Phoenix Force goes underground into a subterranean fortress where they unearth the mastermind, Bruno Carswell. In a blazing firestorm, the fearsome five-man army pulverize Carswell—just in time to prevent a second Korean war!

Watch for new Phoenix Force titles
wherever paperbacks are sold.

HE'S EXPLOSIVE.
HE'S UNSTOPPABLE.
HE'S MACK BOLAN!

learned his deadly skills in Vietnam…then put them to use by destroying Mafia in a blazing one-man war. Now **Mack Bolan** is back to battle new eats to freedom, the enemies of justice and democracy—and he's recruited me high-powered combat teams to help. **Able Team**—Bolan's famous Death uad, now reborn to tackle urban savagery too vicious for regular law orcement. And **Phoenix Force**—five extraordinary warriors handpicked Bolan to fight the dirtiest of anti-terrorist wars around the world.

Fight alongside these three courageous forces for freedom in all-new, lse-pounding action-adventure novels! Travel to the jungles of South America, e scorching sands of the Sahara and the desolate mountains of Turkey. d feel the pressure and excitement building page after page, with nonstop tion that keeps you enthralled until the explosive conclusion! Yes, Mack Bolan d his combat teams are living large…and they'll fight against all odds to otect our way of life!

ow you can have all the new Executioner novels delivered right to ur home!

ou won't want to miss a single one of these exciting new action-adventures. d you don't have to! Just fill out and mail the coupon following and we'll enter ur name in the Executioner home subscription plan. You'll then receive ur brand-new action-packed books in the Executioner series every other onth, delivered right to your home! You'll get two **Mack Bolan** novels, one ble Team and one **Phoenix Force**. No need to worry about sellouts at bookstore…you'll receive the latest books by mail as soon as they come off e presses. That's four enthralling action novels every other month, featuring all ree of the exciting series included in The Executioner library. Mail the card day to start your adventure.

REE! Mack Bolan bumper sticker.

hen we receive your card we'll send your four explosive Executioner ovels and, absolutely FREE, a Mack Bolan "Live Large" bumper sticker! This rge, colorful bumper sticker will look great on your car, your bulletin board, or nywhere else you want people to know that you like to "Live Large." And you are nder no obligation to buy anything—because your first four books come on a)-day free trial! If you're not thrilled with these four exciting books, just return em to us and you'll owe nothing. The bumper sticker is yours to keep, FREE!

Don't miss a single one of these thrilling novels…mail the card now, while ou're thinking about it. And get the Mack Bolan bumper sticker FREE!

BOLAN FIGHTS AGAINST ALL ODDS TO DEFEND FREEDOM

Mail this coupon today!

Gold Eagle Reader Service, a division of Worldwide Library
In U.S.A.: 2504 W. Southern Avenue, Tempe, Arizona 85282
In Canada: 649 Ontario Street, Stratford, Ontario N5A 6W2

FREE! MACK BOLAN BUMPER STICKER
when you join our home subscription plan.

YES, please send me my first four Executioner novels, and include my FREE
Mack Bolan bumper sticker as a gift. These first four books are mine to examine free
10 days. If I am not entirely satisfied with these books, I will return them within 10 day
and owe nothing. If I decide to keep these novels, I will pay just $1.95 per book (total
$7.80). I will then receive the four new Executioner novels every other month as soon
as they come off the presses, and will be billed the same low price of $7.80 per ship-
ment. I understand that each shipment will contain two Mack Bolan novels, one Able
Team and one Phoenix Force. There are no shipping and handling or any other hidden
charges. I may cancel this arrangement at any time, and the bumper sticker is mine to
keep as a FREE gift, even if I do not buy any additional books.

NAME _____ (PLEASE PRINT)

ADDRESS _____ APT. NO

CITY _____ STATE/PROV. _____ ZIP/POSTAL CODE

Signature _____ (If under 18, parent or guardian must sign.) 166–BPM–PAC

This offer limited to one order per household. We reserve the right to exercise discretion in
granting membership. If price changes are necessary, you will be notified.
Offer expires June 30, 1984